"Veering away from the politico and drug culture so prominent in youth pictures . . . JEREMY is a simple love story between two teenagers . . . done with modesty and the right flair . . . handled with touching ability . . ."
—Variety

For young people, for loving people, for everyone who remembers . . .

JEREMY

A novel of awakening first love

ELLIOTT KASTNER
presents
JEREMY

Written and Directed by
ARTHUR BARRON

Starring
ROBBY BENSON

Introducing
GLYNNIS O'CONNOR

Music by
LEE HOLDRIDGE

Produced by
GEORGE PAPPAS

A KENASSET FILM PRODUCTION

UNITED ARTISTS
Entertainment from Transamerica Corporation

Jeremy

By John Minahan

BANTAM BOOKS · TORONTO · LONDON · NEW YORK

A NATIONAL GENERAL COMPANY

$$\text{RLI:} \frac{\text{VLM 3 (VLR 4–5)}}{\text{IL 8–adult}}$$

JEREMY
A Bantam Book / published November 1973

Published simultaneously in the United States and Canada

Bantam Books are published by Bantam Books, Inc., a National
General company. Its trade-mark, consisting of the words "Bantam
Books" and the portrayal of a bantam, is registered in the United
States Patent Office and in other countries. Marca Registrada.
Bantam Books, Inc., 666 Fifth Avenue, New York N.Y. 10019.

PRINTED IN THE UNITED STATES OF AMERICA

For
ARTHUR BARRON
and
DORE SCHARY

For the first time, the first,
I laid my heart open to the
benign indifference of the universe.

Albert Camus

JEREMY.

1

It all happened that crazy autumn when the leaves fell early. I remember there was a sudden cold snap in September, just after school began, and the leaves of the trees in Central Park turned color very quickly. They were bright and lovely in dying, and when Indian summer came, around World Series time, the park was already covered with leaves, and the wind blew swirls of them down across the walkways. All the trees were ragged and fragile, and then finally bare and proud and cold in the sun, and I felt somehow cheated that the summer was gone. It was like the feeling I used to get listening to Tchaikovsky, who was my favorite then, his *Fifth Symphony,* for example, when I was get so deeply lost in the first three movements that the finale always came as a shock. Or listening to the Boston Symphony Orchestra up at Tanglewood, lying on the grass and looking at the stars: I would be off in another dimension in time and space, feeling those emotions that reality would destroy.

That was the year my father accused me of being a

1

dreamer. Among other things. He suggested that I get my head together and get a job after school hours to help pay for my music lessons. About the only thing I could find was a job walking dogs for Budd's Dog Watchers. It didn't pay much, but I love animals, especially dogs, and I took them to the park every afternoon, usually the same ones, in groups of four to six. They would romp in the leaves, and often I'd find myself being pulled all over Sheep Meadow. I knew them all by name, of course; they became my special friends, and sometimes, when they were tired, I'd sit down and read poetry to them. They could be very vocal critics, but their eyes told me they understood. Besides, I couldn't get anyone else to listen. If my father had ever found out I read poetry to dogs, he'd have had an instant laundry problem.

But he was right about the daydreaming; I couldn't seem to concentrate on anything that year. I remember when I made the trip from our West Side apartment out to Brighton Beach on Saturdays for my music lesson, the subway ride was so boring that sometimes I just drifted through the motions automatically, lugging my cello, almost completely oblivious to reality. I would be sitting there, staring out the window, but my mind just refused to be there. Until about an hour later, when the train shot suddenly into daylight, out along the south shore of Coney Island. Daylight would shock me into reality.

I suppose that ride was simply too depressing for a fifteen-year-old mind: the inside of the subway car, like all the others, covered with graffiti that had been sprayed on the walls, windows, doors, even seats. The deafening noise. People reading newspapers or staring into space. Who needed that kind of reality? But when you finally emerged from darkness into daylight that hurt, at least you could smell fresh air again and catch glimpses of the sea down the long narrow streets.

In the autumn, even my music teacher, Max Eisenstein, began to hassle me about daydreaming. I mean he didn't yell at me or anything like that; he never did. But one Saturday he got to me just the same. He was a dynamite guy and I loved him, but this time he hurt me and he did it purposely.

His apartment was near the beach, and he was high up, with a terrific view of the sea. His living room seemed smaller than it really was because it was lined to the ceiling with bookcases and cluttered with paintings and photographs of composers and musicians. He even had sculptures of them. It was a somber room, severe, just like Max. The only thing that wasn't gaunt and serious about Max was his nose. It absolutely dominated his face and put Golda Meir's to shame.

Anyway, this particular morning I was trying my best to concentrate on the music, but I guess my mind was wandering again, because Max interrupted me.

"Jeremy," he said in his quiet way. "Let me ask you something. I'm a little puzzled." He sat forward, blinking, trying to find the words. "How far do you want to get with this? I mean how good do you want to get?"

"I want to be able to play pretty good."

He nodded gravely, took a deep breath. "You know you'll never be concert quality. You know that, don't you?"

"Why not?" I took off my glasses and he went blurred.

"Your energies are too divided. Great musicians save all their energy for their work."

3

"I work hard at my music. You know that."

"Look, I'm not finding fault with you. I just think you're at a point in your studies where you ought to know where I think you stand. There's nothing wrong with being just a *good* musician. You don't have to be *great*. Not everybody can be great."

I thought about it. "I'd like to be."

After our lesson, we took our usual stroll along the boardwalk. Quite a few elderly people were taking the sun, sitting at the edge of the boardwalk on benches overlooking the wide beach. Max tried to cheer me up after what he had said, but he wasn't very good at that kind of thing.

"Well, look," he told me. "Perhaps I was a little harsh with you today. But music is harsh; art is harsh. Standards are high. My standards for you and all my students are high. So, if I have to sacrifice a little warmth in the way I talk to you, you mustn't think that's a lack of affection."

I stopped and looked at him. "Sure. I understand."

"Do you?"

"I think so." I tried to smile.

"I hope so." He smiled too, then glanced away. "Sometimes I think it's a lot easier to be a friend than a teacher."

I worked much harder on my music after that, but I also had a lot of school work to do. I was a sophomore then at the School of Performing Arts over on West Forty-sixth Street. It was a vocational high school, but it was controlled by the City Board of Education, so I had to take a lot of academic courses in addition to music. I didn't really like the academic stuff very much, but I managed to get good grades. I just memorized things, like everybody else.

4

I remember one evening, not long after that talk with Max, I was studying in my room when my father came in. I didn't hear him at first because I had my stereo earphones on, listening to rock.

He startled me when he took them off from behind.

"Oh, hi, Dad."

He just stood there for a moment, looking down at me, pushing back his dark hair, trying to keep his temper. My father was a powerfully built man, maybe a little overweight, and his face always looked tired at night. He was assistant vice-president of advertising and sales promotion at International Airways and had held that job for eight of his twenty-two years with the firm. Which was really something at International, because the pressure at his level had a way of keeping people permanently uptight, even if you had a reputation for pissing ice water. Which was the reputation he had. He could walk a tightrope between creative men and account reps, between last-minute rejections and media deadlines, between imaginative campaigns and Mickey Mouse budgets, between scared men and scared men. Every problem was laid squarely in his lap—emergency, crisis, complicated, expensive. And he could do it. He could piss ice water in a steam bath.

"What are you doing?" he asked softly.

"Homework."

He glanced at the earphones. "How can you possibly work with that thing blaring in your ears?"

"It's easy."

"What do you mean, *easy*? You can't do two things at the same time and do them both well."

"Dad, music helps me to concentrate."

"Ridiculous!" He shook his head, sat down slowly on my bed. "What do you think would happen if everyone in the world tried to do two things at the same time?"

I tried not to smile. "They'd probably get a lot more things done."

"That's not funny. Son, be serious." He got up, walked to my desk and sat on the edge. "We've been over this so many times. Look, everybody works; everybody has a job. My job is advertising. Your job is school."

I was playing with a pencil and he grabbed it from my hand.

"Look at me when I'm talking to you. I've gotten where I am by working hard, by concentrating. And you've got to do the same. You have to concentrate, too."

"But, Dad, I got straight A's, except for one B."

"That's beside the point!" He blurted it out defensively, then glanced down at my open book. "What're you reading?"

"History."

"Well, music and history don't mix." He slid off the desk and started to leave.

"How about music and English?"

He knew I meant it as a gag, but I think he was just too tired to play the game. "How about *English* and English?"

At dinner that night, he was in a slightly better mood because he'd had a couple of drinks, but I could tell that my mother was boring the hell out of him, droning on about some colored tiles she was trying to select for the kitchen floor. It's hard to describe my mother with real objectivity because I was an only child and extremely close to her. But for some reason I remember her vividly that particular evening, her dark hair worn bouffant, skillfully treated, the coloring difficult to detect. Her face seemed almost unlined in that soft light, but her hands were another story.

Right after dinner she placed several sample tiles on the table and studied them. They all looked about the same to me. She lifted her cigarette from the ashtray, took a puff, then put on her glasses and inspected each tile closely.

"Okay, Ben," she said. "I'll explain it to you again. The orange blossom and the caribbean orange both sell for fifteen cents a tile, including installation. The others sell for ten cents a tile, but installation is extra. On the other hand, Marty says this room cries for avocado."

Dad sipped his coffee. "Who's Marty?"

"You know, Ruth's friend, the decorator."

He frowned. "I didn't know we were using a decorator. Since when are we paying for a decorator?"

"Ben, I can't get these tiles without a decorator. Now pick the one you like best and I'll tell you the one I like."

I looked at Dad and crossed my eyes. "Why don't you pick the orange one?"

"Don't be a smart ass."

"But, Dad, they all look the same to me."

Mother narrowed her eyes. "Well, I prefer the carribbean orange. It's happier."

"Happier." I knew damn well I was going to burst out laughing if I didn't leave the table quickly. I got up, said, "Excuse me," as I went into the kitchen.

"Happier than *what*?" Dad asked her. "Which one *is* it?"

"Oh, there's pie in the icebox," she called to me. For some reason she always called it an icebox.

"What kind?"

"When you open the icebox, you'll find out. And, hey, watch out for my plants." She handed Dad the tile. "It's this one, Ben."

"The boy's right. Damn things all look alike."

"To you, I suppose they do."

She was often like that at home. In retrospect, I can understand why, although I could only dimly sense it then. That six-room apartment at 400 West End Avenue was very much her world; she had been in it for most of her adult life. Dad and I operated in worlds vastly different from hers, and I don't think either of us gave that fact very much thought. We woke up in the morning, had a quick breakfast on weekdays, left her there, then appeared again in the late afternoon or early evening, watched the news or studied, talked with her at dinner, watched more television and went to bed. I suppose it had all been different for her when I was a small child, before school; but after that, everything had changed. Oh, she had her own friends, she got out of there often enough, but it wasn't the same.

I'm not saying this was unusual, I'm just saying how it actually was. From the time I entered high school, I didn't talk with her a hell of a lot, or with Dad, either. There wasn't anything as dramatic as a generation gap between us (God, how I hate that term), I just wanted to be left alone more than before. I was changing so quickly that I suppose it was hard for me to digest it all, much less talk about it. They knew that. I'm sure they knew it.

But there were the trips and they helped us all immensely. Far more than I realized at the time. My father's seniority with the airline entitled him to a full month's vacation, which he usually split into two or three shorter holidays, and of course we were all eligible to travel on his passes. I was definitely spoiled in this regard because by the age of fifteen I had literally been around the world twice, visited most of the major cities and took it all pretty much for granted. Airline brats tend to do this. Travel doesn't necessarily make them any wiser, but it gives them a lot of hard knowledge they wouldn't pick up in a classroom, along with a heady feeling of freedom which they haven't earned. Where will we go this time? Acapulco? Rome? Tahiti? Jamaica? It's unreal, but airline people can do it. And most families take advantage of the opportunity, if they can afford the ground expenses. We could. Sometimes we even took weekend trips to relatively faraway places. That is, when Dad wasn't too tired.

Anyway, to get back to that particular evening, after I finished my homework, I decided to practice on the cello before turning in. I could do that in the evenings without disturbing my parents or the neighbors because our apartment building was one of the old ones, constructed in the thirties and really built, with very thick plaster walls and ceilings that were about as close to soundproof as you could get in any apartment. Even our doors were far more solid than in the new buildings.

I remember I was playing an arrangement for cello of Mozart's *Requiem Mass,* the work that Max and I loved so much. It's difficult to explain, but that particular composition always moved and calmed me at the same time. It was Mozart's last work; he did it on commission from a wealthy nobleman, and went back to it time and time again, working feverishly to finish it, with the suspicion that it would be his last work, his own Requiem—which it turned out to be. He died before it was done, and it was completed by his student, Franz Sussmayr. That's the reason my mind gives for my reacting so strongly to it, but when I actually hear it, what I respond with is my emotions. And I dream. For me, the *Requiem Mass* invariably conjures up vivid images of the Egyptian Museum in Cairo, which I had seen when I was quite young, before the Arab-Israeli conflict, back when it was still simple to get into the country. And as I played the music that evening in my room, the familiar images returned to me, without even trying to recall them.

I was again on the second floor of the museum, where the Tutankhamen collection spreads through twelve large rooms. Walking along cool marble corridors, all but deserted that day, high ceilings, windows, dust in long sun-shafts, stillness, my footsteps echoing past royal statues, thrones, showcases, immense gilded wooden cupboards, into Room 4—the exhibits of his tomb from the Valley of the Kings. In the middle, in the glass case, the famed solid gold mask inlaid with deep blue lapis lazuli and bearing Tutankhamen's haunting features: a face not yet twenty, eyes black, lids blue and slanted back to the temples, staring coldly out from a distance of 3,300 years. Against the wall to the right, his first and innermost coffin of solid gold, placed over his mummy and mask; to the left, his second and third gold-plated wooden coffins, covered over with precious stones. And the room down the hall that you had to pay extra to see: a room filled with modern rectangular glass cases, bright, antiseptic almost, sealed, airtight, guarded, twenty glass cases neatly arranged and labeled, an open yellow box in each case, polished wood, white mattress inside each, holding the mummies. Ramses III, shoulders and head unwrapped, face intact, unbelievably red-black skin taut over the skull, veins bulging, hair clinging in back, nose bent down by wrappings, mouth slightly open, teeth showing, sunken eyes staring blankly. Most of the other heads were wrapped, so I kept going back to him. The face wasn't painful to look at, after the initial shock. He had a rather restful expression, like a very old man who had fallen asleep, serenely confident of victory over death, as Pharaohs always were. Immortality was not frightening to them.

"Jeremy," my father's voice called, and I was in my room again, turning to see his silhouette in the now opened doorway. He would do that in the evenings sometimes, just open my door quietly and stand there listening to the music, feeling mellow with his after-dinner drinks. I always played with my back to the door, facing my music stand, and there were times when he would really startle me that way; but I wasn't allowed to lock the door.

"We're going to bed now," he told me softly. "I think it's about time for you, too."

"Oh, okay." I smiled. "Did you finally settle on the caribbean orange?"

He returned the smile wearily, then glanced at his watch. "Come on, it's almost eleven."

I nodded, put my cello and bow aside and gathered up the sheet music. He remained in the doorway as I stood up and went to the closet.

"So you still want to be a musician," he said.

"Yes."

"Why you want to be a musician?"

"I told you. I love music."

"Yeah, well, you can listen to music any time you want to. You can go to concerts and all. I thought you'd grown out of that stage by now."

"It's not a stage, Dad."

He came into the room then, a little unsteadily, sat on my bed and rattled the ice in his glass. "Musicians don't make much money, you know. I mean especially on cello. Have any idea what your average cello player makes in a top symphony orchestra?"

I sat down on the floor, cross-legged, and looked up at him. "He wouldn't be average if he was with a top symphony."

"Just answer the question."

"I don't know," I said very softly.

"Huh? Didn't hear you."

"I don't know what they make. I don't care."

"You don't *care*?" He laughed quietly. "You don't care. Wait'll you're married. You'll *care,* all right."

"I couldn't marry anyone who cared about that."

"Uh-huh. You got all the answers, as usual."

We could hear distant horns from the street. I remember looking out the window at the lights in the apartment building across the street and wishing he'd leave me alone.

"Come on, let's get some sleep," I said, standing. "We're both tired. I just don't want to talk about it."

He was staring at the doorway, his profile yellow in the lamplight. His eyes had filled.

"Oh, Dad," I said softly. "I didn't mean to argue with you, I'm sorry. I always do that when I'm tired, you know that."

12

He turned and looked at me, blinking, shaking his head.

I moved over beside him, feeling so close to tears that I wasn't able to speak. The words just couldn't get out. So I turned my head, picked out a staring point on the floor and stared at it. And then, finally, I tested my throat, my voice, my insides, by making a little half-hum, half-cough, which I had to hear to convince myself that it was all right, that everything would be fine if I kept my voice at that low pitch, that sound that didn't have a shake in it.

"Dad, I don't have any of the answers. I don't know anything, except just one thing. When I'm playing my music, I'm me."

2

One particular day in October stands out vividly in my mind because afterward nothing was really the same. I was heavily into music, which occupied a lot of my time, so I don't think it was so unusual that at fifteen I hadn't yet shown an active interest in girls. That's not to say they didn't turn me on. They did, especially the girls at school. But they always seemed to hang out in groups, at least the ones my age, and that autumn they all looked about the same to me, probably because most of them dressed alike and almost all of them had long hair. They tended to blur together. In retrospect, I think I was mostly attracted to the *idea* of girls. It was pleasant to watch them and to entertain the usual harmless fantasies. I never admitted it to anyone, much less to myself, but I suppose I was afraid of them, afraid of rejection and embarrassment and getting hurt. I had a definite gut feeling of inferiority around girls. I felt that I was just plain unattractive. I wore heavy glasses, I was painfully shy, awkward as hell, and I absolutely blew it every time I tried to talk with a girl. Needless to say, I had never tried to ask for a date. The thought entered my mind a few times, but I simply couldn't cut it.

Anyway, I remember we were tuning up before music class—two girl violinists, a boy violist, and me on the cello—when the teacher came in. His name was Mr. Howard, a young guy and about as inexperienced and nervous as they come, but I liked him.

"Good morning, class," he began in his uncertain way. "Uh, I'd like to have your attention now for a few minutes. The concert has definitely been scheduled to take place in two weeks."

There were groans from all over the room.

"Uh-huh, in two weeks. Not much time, but we'll be all right. Now, Diane and Sherry are scheduled to begin the program, so if we could have something from them to begin the class with . . ."

Diane and Sherry started playing a rather difficult violin duet, concentrating intently. I knew I'd be next, so I had the usual butterflies and my hands began to sweat. That always happened, whether I was playing in front of Max, a class or an audience. I couldn't seem to shake it.

When the girls had finished, Mr. Howard hesitated, as usual, as if not knowing what to say. He didn't exactly inspire a hell of a lot of confidence.

"Very good. You've been working," he told them, finally. "It was good on the sec—on the first part; the second half we're going to have to work on. Got plenty of time to take care of that. Very good. Thank you." He smiled, then hesitated. "All right, now let's have Jeremy. All right, are we ready, Jeremy? Take it."

I'd selected one of my favorites for the concert, the cello part from Beethoven's *Quartet*, opus 59, no. 3, a major work in the cello repertory which involves playing scales in broken thirds instead of in the less difficult consecutive steps. To minimize rearranging the fingering patterns, I used extension fingerings. This saves time and unnecessary motions. In other words, I didn't move the first finger until it was time to shift the entire hand. The selection was a challenge for me and I enjoyed it. I closed my eyes during several passages and tried to feel the emotion that had gone into its creation. I loved Beethoven. I loved his feeling.

"That's very nice, Jeremy," Mr. Howard said, after a pause. "Did you hear that, class? Now, that cello piece is usually played as part of a quartet, with the slow passages counterpointed by staccato sixteenth notes in the violas. Here, let me show you on the blackboard." He turned to the blackboard, looked around for the chalk, couldn't find any. "There's no chalk. Jeremy, will you please get me some chalk?"

"Sure." I stood up, went to the door.

As I walked down the long corridor, I could hear the start of more ensemble music from the class, but when I went downstairs, it was replaced by the more graceful piano music of a ballet, undoubtedly a recording. I wasn't exactly sure where it was coming from until I passed the open door of the room and saw the girl. I remember she was wearing a black leotard and had her leg up on the bar, bending her body toward it.

Something about that glimpse made me stop and go back. I looked into the room and saw her practicing alone at the bar on the wall in front of a large mirror, absorbed in the music. Then I saw my own reflection with a shock—thick glasses, pale face, unruly hair, tall

17

and awkward—and for a split second my mind snapped back ten full months to the identical image that was frozen in my memory with such mixed emotions. Bangkok in December, dining with Mother and Dad at the Sbai-thong in Rajaprasong near Klong Mana Nak, our shoes carefully removed by the two kneeling men at the door. Upstairs you sat cross-legged on blue Thai-silk cushions at the long low tables in candlelight, where most of the diners were American soldiers on R and R without dates, where young Thai girls knelt down at your table with hands in the praying posture before serving the six Siamese dishes circling the basic rice and Mother showed me how you ate them clockwise and individually, from the burning-hot egg soup to the cooling shrimp; tea and the *pee-bhat* music starting up softly, as corner lights dimmed and the small floor-level stage brightened into a pool of yellow for the full-dress Khon and Lakorn-ram classical dances, all mute except for the clack of sticks in the Phra-ram and Asura duel. Afterward, the quiet announcement that four of the girls would come out to select partners for lessons on stage, and the gentle girl walking directly toward me and smiling only at me and kneeling before me, with her hands praying.

May I have the honor of teaching you in dance
Oh I appreciate it but listen I'm a terrible—
Oh Jeremy go ahead go ahead
—dancer listen I think the men at the next—
Jeremy it'll be fun go ahead
—table would love to be asked they'd be much—
Please may I have the honor

18

—better at it no really I'd rather not
Jeremy you'll hurt her feelings go ahead
Please come I have selected you
I can't really please ask the servicemen they'd—
Please come the music has started
Jeremy you'll hurt her feelings
Yes all right okay thank you I just—

Then to the stage, and immediately dancing in a circle with the girls between us and showing finger positions and hand movements to laughter from the crowd, and the three bull-like soldiers with short haircuts laughing, too (I was sure they were all laughing at me); but we couldn't see the audience, only our reflections in the large, mirrored backdrop panels and the panic in my face.

Instantly, I was back at the door of the classroom, looking at the same panicked face in the mirror. I glanced away quickly. The girl in the black leotard continued her dance, lost in the music, thick brunette hair swirling back over her shoulders now, almost reaching her waist.

She stopped abruptly when she saw me in the mirror. Her face was lovely and frightened. "Oh! Oh, you scared me!"

"Oh, gee . . . I'm sorry."

As she leaned over to turn off the stereo set, her hair fell forward. She pushed it back when she turned, revealing an oval face with a rather high forehead, almost transparent blue eyes, full lips. A sensitive face.

"You really scared me," she said in a much softer voice.

"Oh, I . . . I'm sorry."

19

"What are you doing here?"

"I don't know . . . uh . . . oh, I was walking by this door, and I . . . I saw you dancing."

I remember her looking up at me, nodding.

I was so spaced out I simply didn't know what to say. "Hey, that thing you were doing, that was a *plié*, right?"

"What makes you think that was a *plié*?"

"I don't know." I had to smile. "It's the only dance word I know."

"Well, it wasn't."

"Oh."

She seemed to look right through me. "What do you want?"

I glanced around. "Uh . . . is there any chalk in here?"

"Yeah, there's some over there."

"Oh. Yeah." I saw it, but I couldn't move.

"You'll have to excuse me. I've got to get this thing together. I'm being tested in a few minutes."

"Oh, yeah. Sure, go ahead."

She leaned over and turned on the music again. I started to leave.

"Nice meeting you," she said.

I stopped, surprised. "Yeah, sure."

I recall walking down the corridor in a real daze. Before I got back to my music class, I realized that I hadn't taken the chalk. I had to find another empty classroom to get some, and it took a while. When I returned, Mr. Howard asked why I'd been gone so long and I couldn't think of an answer. I just stood there, shrugging my shoulders; I was too preoccupied even to lie. The class had a good laugh. I found out later that they thought I'd gone to the bathroom and that I was too embarrassed to tell him. Then I really *was* embarrassed.

I didn't tell anybody about the girl until I saw Ralph Manzonni later that morning. Ralph was my best friend, but we were about as different as you could get when it came to girls. He was so cool with girls, I couldn't believe it. It was an education to see him operate. He wasn't exactly handsome, but he was well built and a good athlete, and the girls around school really seemed to dig him. It was the way he handled himself, his style. He had a lot of confidence.

I met him outside the library and we walked down the corridor. I could hardly wait to tell him, to share it with somebody.

"Ralphy, she's beautiful."

"What're you talking about? Who's beautiful?"

"Oh, man, there's this new girl at school, a dancer. I can't believe it."

"You met a girl today?"

"I was going past this room to get a piece of chalk, and there was this girl dancing there."

He gave me a look. "Jesus."

"Oh, wow. She's unreal."

"What's her name?"

I stopped dead. "Oh, shit."

"You didn't get her *name*?"

"Oh, God, I blew it."

We continued down the corridor in silence, Ralph glancing at me and shaking his head.

"How do you ask a girl her name?"

He looked at the ceiling and made a soft whistle. "How do you ask her her name? Oh, that's simple. You just go up to her and start a conversation with her. And after a while . . ."

That was typical of the advice he always gave me. It seemed so easy to him.

After school, I walked the dogs in Central Park again. It was pleasantly cool and the park was bright with leaves. Kids were playing football all over, and I remember there was a faint smell of leaves burning from somewhere. When the dogs were tired enough, I called a rest in the middle of Sheep Meadow and decided to share my news by reading some poetry to them. I finally selected something from Wordsworth that seemed appropriate to my mood, *"She Was a Phantom of Delight,"* just a few lines of it.

> She was a phantom of delight
> When first she gleamed upon my sight;
> A lovely apparition, sent
> To be a moment's ornament;
> Her eyes as stars of twilight fair,
> Like twilight's, too, her dusky hair,
> But all things else about her drawn
> From May-time and the cheerful dawn.

Most of my friends back then thought Wordsworth was kind of corny; so did the dogs. But I liked him. I told the dogs that I was considering reading them a haiku poem on obedience the next day.

But after school the next day, I talked Ralph into walking the dogs for me. I decided that I absolutely had to see the girl again. Not to say anything to her. I wasn't ready for that. I simply wanted to see her, to observe her, to be reasonably close to her. It probably sounds dumb, but I wanted to see how she walked and moved, how she wore her hair, how she reacted to things, how she looked in street clothes. So I just waited outside school that afternoon, a safe distance from the front entrance, determined to spot her.

Well, I swear to God, she must have been the last girl to come out. When I had just about decided that I'd missed her, out she came, alone, passing quickly through the gang of kids who always hung around in front, and heading in the opposite direction from where I was standing. I remember the excitement I felt just seeing her. The street was fairly crowded at that time of day and I kept a good distance behind her, always letting about ten people separate us. When she had to wait for the traffic light to change at the corner of West Forty-sixth and Fifth Avenue, I slowed up considerably, then had a good view as she crossed. She was shorter than I remembered, very slim, her hair long and loose, parted in the middle, and she was constantly tossing it back over her shoulders. She wore a blue workshirt—with the tails out—as a kind of jacket over her red T-shirt, and her red belled corduroys sort of scuffed on the street as she walked. It may seem crazy, but I followed her for about two hours that afternoon, first into a record store, then into three department stores. I was positive she didn't see me and I quit while I was ahead.

But the next morning, I was watching her again, in the school library this time, at closer range. She was about four tables away, near the window, and Ralph was at my table. We were pretending to concentrate on our books.

"Ridiculous, man," Ralph said very softly. "You've been

following her and all. Why don't you just go up and ask her out?"

"I can't do that."

"What do you mean, you can't do that?"

"I don't know. I'm just not ready yet. Hey, look, this is okay for now. I just like being near her."

He grabbed at his hair. "You like being near her. Then why're we sitting back here and she's sitting up there? I don't get it."

"She'll never go out with me."

"How do you know if you don't ask her?"

"Her friends would probably laugh at her if she went out with a sophomore."

He smiled, nodded. "Tell her you got left back."

I took him seriously. "No, I couldn't do that. Then she'd think I'm stupid. Hey, look. Next period is lunch, I'll talk to her then."

I remember the school cafeteria was crowded and noisy and we had difficulty spotting her. She was sitting alone at the end of one of the long tables, eating a sandwich. Ralph wanted us to go up and sit right next to her, but I persuaded him to sit about three tables away. It was the first time I had seen her in the cafeteria, and I had a good view of her right profile, or what I could see of it with the long hair. Ralph kept urging me to go ahead and I kept putting him off with the excuse that I had to eat something first. Then I just couldn't do it. I couldn't go up to her. Finally, when she was almost finished, Ralph started to burn.

"I can't," I told him. "I can't."

"If you don't go up there, *I'm* going up there. I mean it."

"Will you cut it out!"

"If you don't go up there by the time I count to ten, I'm going up there and *I'll* speak to her."

That got me really uptight. "Please, Ralphy."

"Ten. Nine. Eight."

"Cut it out, will you?"

"Seven. Six. Five."

"Ralphy . . ."

"Four. Three."

"Come on, man."

"Two." He stood up quickly.

"Hey, where you going?"

"One." He left the table and started toward her.

"Come on, man!"

At first I thought he was just going to bluff it, walk right up to her and then go past, but I suppose I should've known better. He sat right next to her, introduced himself and started a conversation. Then he turned and pointed at me.

I didn't even wait for the girl to look at me; I split out of there instantly, trying to walk casually, but feeling a need to run, bumping into people, swearing to myself. Out in the corridor, I didn't know where to go next; my first reaction was to find some room to hide in. But my curiosity was too strong. I walked back to the cafeteria door, opened it and glanced in. Ralph was still talking with her, gesturing with his hands now. I remember feeling so frustrated and embarrassed—and angry at myself —that I walked over to the row of metal wall lockers and punched one of them very hard. My fist ached, but I didn't give a damn.

Then Ralph came through the door, smiling.

"Hey, what did you point at me for?"

He kept smiling—all confidence, as usual. "Come on, take it easy. She wants you to call her."

"Get out of here!"

"Really. I don't know why, but she wants you to call her."

I looked in his eyes. "Really?"

"Yeah. Her name is Susan Rollins. Here's her telephone number." He handed me a scrap of paper with a number.

"Wow. Does she know I'm a sophomore?"

"No. She doesn't know you're a sophomore."

"Oh, great."

"I told her you were a senior."

"You told her I was a *senior*?"

He laughed loudly, shoved me away. "No, I'm only kidding. I just told her that since you were the best musician in school, and I heard she was the best dancer—"

"How do you know she's the best dancer? Hey, Ralphy, you don't know *anything*."

"I don't know anything? I was the one went in there to rap with her, not you. You see, what you needed all along was me." He glanced away. "Oh, there's only one thing. Well, she's wearing this shirt with this guy's name written on it."

I looked at the cafeteria door. "Oh, really? Oh."

"It's got this guy's name written on it, right over the pocket. You know, like those shirts you see in a gas station."

"Really? What does it say?"

"Well, I don't know. I didn't want her to think I was staring at her tits or anything."

I absolutely had to find out so after school that afternoon, Ralph and I waited for her to come out. We were standing with a crowd of kids directly across the street from the entrance and we didn't have to wait long. She appeared at the door together with a big group, but as they started to scatter on the sidewalk, we had a clear look. She wore a faded blue workshirt with a large red name over the left breast pocket: *Cézanne.*

Ralph smiled, shrugged. "It was a guy's name, all right."

I felt so relieved that I wanted to burst out laughing, but within seconds my mood was completely reversed. Some guy came out, called to her, caught up with her and started a conversation. He was a good-looking kid and she seemed to know him very well. They walked off together, talking easily. I remember feeling like someone had just punched me in the stomach.

3

I didn't call her that week or even the next, despite Ralph's continual urging, and I suppose if I'm honest with myself I have to admit that I liked it better that way. She saw a lot of the good-looking guy during that time and they often met after school. I found out his first name was Danny, but that's all I really knew about him, except that he handled himself very smoothly around her and she seemed to like him. In some strange way, that took pressure off me and opened the door again to fantasy, which was familiar and pleasurable and far more secure. The truth is that I didn't really want to meet her, at least not until I got adjusted to the idea. I knew Ralph meant well, aside from the fact that it was an ego trip for him, but he was shoving me along and I just wasn't ready for it.

I saw her often enough around school, I made it a point to find out where and when her classes were, and a few times when we passed in the corridors our eyes met. That was fine for a start and I didn't feel as nervous as I had, thinking that I had to call her and go through the whole thing of asking her for a date. At least she knew my name and what I looked like, and she had asked me to call her, although I suspected that Ralph had twisted her arm a little. And that was enough. I wrote her name on many pages of my notebooks, sometimes making intricate patterns with it, while I daydreamed in class and at home, and I even said her name out loud frequently when I was walking the dogs in the park. I'd just say, "Susan Rollins, Susan Rollins, Susan Rollins," as often as I wanted, soft or loud, scuffing through the leaves on those cool afternoons, and nobody could hear. One day when Danny walked her home, I followed—at a considerable distance—to find out where she lived. It was a five-story townhouse, converted to apartments, at 40 East Seventy-fourth Street, between Park and Madison, a really fashionable area, which led me to believe that her family was probably loaded. But that even heightened my illusions about her. On three occasions I walked past the house in the early evening, first across the street from it, and then twice on the same side—moving quickly, but studying the whole block and even the sidewalk where she walked every day, trying to memorize details about the house. I would look up at the lighted windows, not knowing which floor she was on but imagining how she was at home, studying, having dinner, watching television, and picturing how she looked.

Alone in my room at night, trying to sleep, I would be drawn into the almost inevitable sexual fantasies that I was expected to struggle against by reason of religious tradition—with predictable results. On a very basic level, I think I understood that yielding to desires so strong and persistent had to be considered a real physical necessity, and that prolonged abstention was not going to help matters all that much. But I tried. I tried hard because I was expected to try. The images would come anyway, again and again, and Susan would be there, looking lovely and happy, in sometimes elaborate situations and dialogues, and I would make concentrated efforts not to think about her; sometimes, in desperation, I would ask God for help. But when I gave in, when I was beaten, just before sleep finally came, I would again be haunted by feelings of guilt and shame and remorse, feelings perpetuated by a tradition so utterly outdated that, seen in perspective, its very endurance seems incredible. I would be less than honest if I said that I was not damaged by all that. Someone, anyone, should have had the courage in this day and age to tell me the truth: that neither my parents nor my religion nor my God really held that there was anything shameful or dirty or dishonorable about such a personal physical fact as masturbation and that there was no need for repentance of any kind. Someone should have told me that it was merely a necessary part of my transition to maturity. But nobody had the courage to do that.

Max came the closest to helping me through this period, although I'm sure he didn't know precisely what the problem was. On the Saturday prior to my major school recital, I had my regular music lesson with him in the morning, out at his apartment in Brighton Beach. I was working hard on the Beethoven and I remember I was particularly nervous. When I finished the piece, there was a long silence. Max was sitting on the piano bench across the room, staring out the window.

"What do you think?" I asked.

"Mmm. That's very nice. I don't know why you're so

31

nervous about playing at your school recital." He stood up slowly, walked toward me and sat in a chair opposite. "The problem is in the interpretation, not in the technique."

"The fingering you showed me before, that really helped me a lot."

"Yes, I know. But my value as your teacher is not just to make you a good technician. The emotion is equally important—more important, in fact. I . . . I don't like some of the things you're doing, Jeremy. What do you think about when you're playing this piece?"

"What do you mean?"

"I mean what kind of thoughts go through your mind when you're playing?"

I thought about it. "Well, it's a sad piece. It's kind of lonely."

"Sadness is just part of it. He wrote this piece before he was twenty. He wrote it for a beautiful peasant girl he had seen just once, in passing. Just once. The music expresses love and parting simultaneously. The music expresses *life*. Play it that way!"

He walked back and stood in front of the piano. I tried to concentrate on a happier mood as I played, but it was difficult. The butterflies were there again and my hands were sweating. Finally, I just had to stop.

"I'm sorry," I told him. "I don't know what it is. It's just that sometimes my hand gets sweaty and I can't keep my fingers on the strings."

He nodded. "That's just nervousness. Look, the only way I know to keep from getting nervous is to stare the audience down. Before you start to play, before you even pick up your bow, look out at the audience and don't play a note until there's not a sound in that room. Not a sound. You'll be surprised how fast the nervousness will go away when you're in command."

"I'll try that. I don't know if it's going to work, though."

To say that the recital was an important event in my life would be a fantastic understatement. All of my training in school and private lessons over a period of some four years had been building toward just such an event. The following Friday night I was to be the cello soloist, backed by the entire school orchestra.

As it happened, Dad was at a marketing meeting in London that had long been scheduled for that Thursday and Friday, and although he knew how important it was to me, there was just no way he could make it. Mother and I took a taxi to the school and when we saw the crowd my first reaction was one of absolute panic. The auditorium had a capacity of around two hundred, and when I went out on stage to tune up, with the house lights on, the place was so packed that I couldn't believe it. I mean I knew there would be a good crowd, there always was at those recitals, that's what the school was all about. But I didn't expect near capacity. About five minutes before we started, I couldn't see more than ten empty seats. I scanned the rows for familiar faces, saw Max, my mother, Ralph and most of my teachers. Then I saw Susan. She was up fairly close, about eighth row center, talking with a blond man whom I guessed to be her father. I glanced away instantly, but I felt even more tension. I was separated from the orchestra, out front on my own, with absolutely nowhere to hide.

Anyway, all too soon, the houselights dimmed, and

Mr. Howard, who was conducting that night, tapped his baton for silence; a hush came over the audience very gradually. The piece called for me to start alone, joined later by the orchestra, and I was so nervous that I thought, the hell with it, I'll just stare them down, I'll take command right now, I won't play a note until I have total silence.

I couldn't see the audience by then; they were in virtual darkness except for the dim red glow of the exit signs. But I could hear a few remaining voices, far back to the left. I waited, staring toward the voices. They continued I waited. Mr. Howard tapped his baton again, getting impatient, probably not knowing what to do, but I wouldn't even look at him. I was determined to stare the bastards down. And I did it. It worked. I even waited a few extra beats after I had complete silence, just to punctuate the point. Then I turned to Mr. Howard, took the signal and began.

It was an emotion that's almost impossible to describe, but as soon as I played the first few notes, I experienced a strange calm, a feeling of utter control usually alien to me, and then the music took over and I was lost in it, dreaming memories that only music, music alone, could recall unannounced, from wherever it was inside me that was *me:*

Paris on a weekend at the end of April, when Dad wasn't with us, in a room at Le Bristol overlooking Faubourg St. Honoré and the proud shabby old rooftops with fences and gardens and multiple chimneys and the skylights all colored at night. Mother standing on the little balcony in her blue dressing gown and pearl necklace, smoking, tired from her cold and the trip, a silver cham-

34

pagne bucket on the table near her reflection in the opened balcony doors. Her eyes in the flower market (always that way with flowers) in the red shade of awning, and the new April leaves making web-like sunspots on the walk. Laughing and sad on the Bateaux-Mouche when the old Russian man decided he was happy enough to get up and sing with the orchestra. Leaning forward, hands behind her back, to read the English newspapers in the long glass case outside La Figaro Agricole: my funny-looking mother with the big eyes who had always wanted to be beautiful. The beautiful people would have a free ride all their lives, and most of them would take it for granted, the excitement, the attention, the smiles, the invitations, the competition, all the things she never got, all the things she'd wanted and hoped for. They would never understand the way she did. They would never have the advantage of learning what beauty is. They would never be as beautiful as she was in Paris, wearing her white coat, holding her makeup kit, pausing near the door, looking back at the room for the last time, smiling her tight-lipped smile, and saying gently, almost in a whisper, "I want to remember our little room."

I remained in that dimension throughout the entire recital, oblivious to anything but those visions the music summoned up in me, feeling vibrations of the intangible perhaps more deeply than ever before. When the music ended, there was a moment of silence—a beat, like the drawing of breath—and then I was in reality again, hearing the applause. It came from the darkness and actually startled me, and it got louder, louder when the parents joined in, deeper, stronger, louder when the houselights came on, blinding at first, colors swimming. Louder still when I finally remembered to stand up, blinking, adjusting my glasses, afraid again. I seem to recall bowing stiffly, shaking hands with Mr. Howard and bowing to the orchestra, but I don't even recall walking off stage. It was all a blur until I realized I was leaning against the wall backstage, trying to catch my breath, hearing the applause soften, swell again for a moment and gradually end.

Afterward, everyone milled around in the auditorium lobby to meet other families and exchange congratulations. It was very congested and smoke hung in the air. I finally spotted my mother, who was talking to some woman, and as I maneuvered over to them, Max was suddenly at my side, smiling. He shook my hand with a strong grip.

"Well done," he told me.

"Thank you."

"Very well done, Jeremy." He was really smiling then and his eyes were alive, but I knew he was uncomfortable around all those people. "I'll see you next week, same time." He turned and moved off into the crowd. I had to smile about him. Sometimes he seemed even more shy than I was. I had wanted to talk with him. But at least I knew he was pleased.

Mother started chatting with another woman; I stood to one side.

"Jeremy was wonderful," the woman said.

Mother looked happy. "Thank you very much."

"You must be very proud."

"I am, indeed."

"I'm sorry Mr. Jones wasn't able to come."

"Oh, well, I am too; but he does work very hard, you know."

They went on like that, endlessly, not knowing really what to say to each other, but making the effort, being polite.

Ralph grabbed my arm as he passed. "Great!"

"I'll see you tomorrow."

I was being bumped around in the crowd, still waiting for my mother to stop talking with the woman, when Susan appeared on the other side of them, waiting to move through. She was looking directly at me and holding her gaze steady, but she seemed too shy to come around. I really surprised myself. Instead of glancing away, I thought, Jesus, if I'm ever going to do it, it's got to be now.

"Hi," I said.

She smiled. "I loved your playing."

"Gee, thanks a lot."

"I'm Susan Rollins."

"Yeah, I know."

"You were really good."

"Thanks . . . thanks a lot."

She moved away quickly. "Bye."

"Bye."

That's all there was to it. But as soon as she left, I made up my mind that I'd call her and ask her out. Seeing her like that, talking with her, was actually the highlight of the evening for me, not the recital. I knew I could play well if I put my mind to it, but I was beginning to wonder if I'd ever have the courage to approach her. Now I had it; I had the confidence I needed.

I didn't sleep much that night, thinking about her and how she looked at me, trying to remember exactly what we said to each other and what I'd say when I called. Since I had never asked any girl for a date, it bothered me that I wouldn't know what to say, or that I'd say the wrong thing. I hardly thought about the recital at all. That was already a thing of the past.

When I woke up Saturday morning, I realized that I needed some advice from Ralph. He'd know exactly what to say. I didn't have my regular music lesson with Max, because of the recital, so I called Ralph and we went over to the school gym and played some basketball. Afterwards, we talked in the locker room. I was perfectly honest with him, because I needed straight answers.

"I want to call her, but I don't know what to say."

"Well, how about hello, for a start?"

"Yeah, I know I should say hello. The problem is what comes after hello. I mean, girls like Susan are probably used to talking to guys on the phone. She probably expects me to sound interesting. You know what I mean."

"It's easy, man, really easy."

"Well, give me something to say."

He glanced at me, realizing I was serious. "You don't know what to say?"

"No."

"Okay. Ask her what she did today."

I nodded. " 'What'd you do today?' Yeah, I think that's pretty good. What else?"

"I don't know." He sat down on the bench. "Ask her if she thinks you should paint your cello a different color."

"Come on, man, be serious. What do *you* say to girls when you talk to them on the phone?"

"I usually don't say much. I usually listen. For instance, Laurie. You know that girl Laurie I used to go with, this summer?"

I sat next to him. "Yeah?"

"Honest to God, we used to stay on the phone for hours. All I had to say was, 'uh-huh,' 'really,' 'no kidding.' Man, she used to babble on for hours."

"No, but I kind of think I should say *something*. Hey, what if I made a list?"

He smiled at that. "Yeah, make a list. Oh, yeah, write down everything you have to say. When you finish with the list, hang up!"

He usually put me on like that, but at least he gave me some ideas and got me talking about it. Things like that didn't seem so much of a problem when I talked with Ralph because he had a way of putting them in perspective—often at my expense, but still. He had the right idea; you had to see the humor in it all. I saw the humor, all right, but when you've never asked a girl for a date, somehow the whole process doesn't seem very funny. You have to do it first.

That afternoon, I went home and actually made a list of possible things to say to her, mostly questions, so that the burden of thinking would be hers. Then I wrote out entire sentences that I could just read verbatim. They sounded too formal, so I changed to a more vernacular approach, adding possible replies on her part, followed by my replies to her replies. But that just got too involved, so I decided to go back to a simple list of questions. When I had eliminated all the really dumb stuff and had gotten down to the final draft, I closed my door and started rehearsing out loud. The thing is, I had been yelling during the basketball game that morning and my voice wasn't very good at that point. I was having the usual problems with it that year, anyway, and I knew from experience that any strain would make it unpredictable, which I wasn't about to risk. At any rate, that was the major excuse I gave myself for not calling her that evening.

Sunday morning I got up about seven o'clock, had a quick breakfast alone (Mother and Dad usually slept late on Sunday), and then started rehearsing again in my room, with the door closed, determined to make the call around nine. Certain private moments remain vividly in the mind, recalled by the smallest things, because they are somehow more important than all the major events can ever be. I will never forget sitting on my bed that morning, talking into the receiver while holding the connection button down, trying to make it as realistic as possible.

"Hi, Susan." My voice was too high; I lowered it. "Hello, Susan. I bet you didn't think I would call so fast, huh?"

I slammed the receiver down, walked to my music stand and picked up my final revised list of things to say. I stood in front of the mirror on my closet door.

"Hello, Susan." Not too bad that time. I removed my glasses slowly, assumed a debonair expression, which seemed to help. "This is Jeremy Jones." My voice broke on the surname, as it often did, for some reason. Christ, I thought, if I can't say my own name, I'm in great shape.

But by nine o'clock, I knew I was as ready as I'd ever be. I sat on my bed—telephone in my lap, list beside me —took a deep breath, lifted the receiver and dialed the number. My hands were sweating. As soon as I heard the ringing signal, I whipped off my glasses, tossed them on the bed and clenched my free hand into a tight fist.

It rang about four times.

"Hello," a girl's voice said.

"Uh, hello, Susan, this is Jeremy Jones; I'm sorry I called so early, but like I'm on my way out."

"Wait a minute. This isn't Susan, this is her sister. Just a minute. Susan, it's for you."

I shut my eyes tightly. "Oh."

In the distance, I could hear her sister say, "What *time* is it, anyway?"

I glanced at my watch. Oh, God, I thought. I remember lowering the receiver to my lap as I wiped my forehead.

"Hello?" For just an instant, I didn't know where the voice was coming from. I yanked the receiver back to my ear.

"Hello—oh, hello, Susan—uh, this is Jeremy Jones."

"Oh, hi, Jeremy, how are you?" Her voice sounded cheerful.

"Oh, I'm okay, how are you?"

"Okay."

"Okay. I guess I called a little too early, huh?"

"Oh, no, that's okay."

"Uh—" I picked up the list of questions, realized I didn't have my glasses on, had to squint at the first question: "How are you?"

"Fine."

Christ, I'd already asked that! I grabbed my glasses, put them on, read the second question: "Oh, what did you do today?"

"Umm, I . . . I woke up, I had some orange juice. Jeremy, it's only nine o'clock!"

I decided to skip all the rest and get right to it. "Listen, I know this is a little short notice. Uh—but would you like to go out tonight?"

She hesitated. "Um, tonight . . ."

I assumed rejection, almost with relief. "Look, if you don't want to go out tonight, that's all right."

"No, no, that's okay. Tonight is fine."

"Oh. Uh, great. The movie starts at six and eight."

"Oh, I didn't know we were going to the movies."

"Isn't that all right?"

"Sure." There was a pause. "What movie?"

"*My Little Chickadee,* with W.C. Fields. Is that okay?"

"Yeah. Yeah, sure."

"Oh, good. If we go to the six o'clock show, we'll avoid the lines."

"That's fine with me."

"Okay. Look, I'll have to pick you up around five fifteen, because it's at the Thalia, up at Ninety-fifth and Broadway—you know, the one that specializes in old flicks? And it'll take a little time, even by cab."

"We're going by cab?"

"Sure."

"You don't have to do that, Jeremy."

"No, I want to."

"Okay." Another pause. "You know where I live?"

"Forty East Seventy-fourth."

"Right." There was a smile in her voice. "Third floor."

The rest of the day I felt so excited that I couldn't study, couldn't concentrate on the Sunday *Times,* couldn't even sit still in the living room with my father, watching the football game on television. I remember the Jets were playing the Colts at Baltimore, and Namath was going to the air almost from the opening scrimmage, but I couldn't have cared less.

4

At four o'clock I started to get ready. I took a long
shower, shampooed my hair, put conditioner on it, then
used my mother's small hair dryer. My hair wasn't all
that long, compared to a lot of guys, but it came down
well over my ears, you know, and the dryer gave it a
certain body. After I'd combed it, I used some spray to
keep it reasonably in place. I remember I took a long
time trying on different things and looking at myself in
the mirror. At four forty-five, I was afraid I'd be late if I
took the crosstown bus or tried to walk through the park,
so I took a taxi. I had the driver drop me at the corner
of Madison and Seventy-fourth, because I was about ten
minutes early. I killed time by looking at paintings and
prints and art objects in the windows of the art shops
along Madison. There were dozens of art galleries and
shops in that area. Then I found that instead of looking at
the paintings and stuff, I was staring at my own reflection
in the windows. Despite all my preparations, I was the
same ugly guy, with those thick black-rimmed glasses,
pale face and messed-up hair. The only difference was

that I looked very scared, which I was. I could feel it down in my stomach and my hands were sweating and I felt out of breath.

Anyway, at about ten past five, I walked nonchalantly down Seventy-fourth Street, taking deep breaths like they tell you to do in basketball when you're on the freethrow line. It's supposed to have a calming effect and loosen you up, but I swear to God, it seemed to have just the opposite effect on me that afternoon. When I saw the two white pillars at the entrance to 40, my hands and legs began to shake. I don't mean tremble, I mean they literally shook. My face felt almost paralyzed. I couldn't believe it. It was like I was inside someone else's body and I couldn't control it.

Somehow, I went in the outside door, which was unlocked, looked for "Rollins" on the listings next to the bells and pressed the right button. I remember my hand was visibly shaking when I did that. I started to take more deep breaths, but the buzzer on the inside door blasted so loudly, it scared the shit out of me. For just an instant, I didn't know what was happening; then I grabbed for the inside door handle. I was a split second too late; the buzzer had stopped.

"You *shit!*" I said to the handle, twisting it with both hands then, trying to force it.

Then I had to face the humiliation of ringing the bell again. I knew they'd think I was a real idiot, but I had no choice, so I rang it again, very briefly, then shot quickly to the inside door and got my hand on the knob. The buzzer blasted again, longer this time, and I pushed hard and stepped into the small, dimly lighted lobby. I waited a few seconds for my eyes to adjust, then looked around for an elevator. There wasn't any, just a big red-carpeted staircase. I walked slowly to the third floor, pausing to take deep breaths at every landing. Everything was very quiet. There were two apartments to each floor, front and back, with polished wooden doors, and thick red carpeting everywhere.

The Rollins had the front apartment on the third floor, with a little nameplate over the bell. I took a swipe at my hair, dried my hands on my sweater and pressed the button. I could hear it ring inside. Within seconds, I heard heavy footsteps approaching on a bare wood floor. The door swung open and her father greeted me, the man with the blond hair I had seen with her at the concert.

"Hi, Jeremy, I'm Ned Rollins," he said warmly, extending his hand.

"Oh, hi, Mr. Rollins."

As I reached for his hand, I just missed a solid connection, so that he wound up shaking my fingers. It happened very fast, of course, and then we were inside and he was closing the door, but I will never forget the slight flicker of diasppointment in his eyes when he shook my fingers, like he thought I was a fag or something, and I knew there was nothing I could do to change that impression right away; that would have to wait. It was out of the question to make a joke out of it, because I was so unnerved I didn't trust my voice, much less my sense of humor.

We walked down the hallway toward the living room.

"You were really excellent at the school concert the other night," he told me.

"Oh, thank you."

"Really excellent. We thought the whole thing was superbly done."

"Oh, thanks."

The living room was large and tastefully decorated, overlooking the street. I remember expensive-looking furniture, oil paintings and a black marble fireplace. The draperies were open to fading sunlight, warming the colors in the big Oriental rug and casting rectangles of light across the dark wood floor.

"This is very nice," I said.

He nodded, motioning for me to sit on the long white couch. "Susan'll be out in a minute. Sit down. Can I offer you a Coke or something?"

"Oh, no. No, thank you."

He sat in an armchair nearby, and as he lit a cigarette, I took my first good look at him. His blond hair was neatly combed and not too long, with a single lock falling over his high forehead, and he was lean and almost rugged looking in a crew-neck sweater, jeans and beat-up loafers. But there was a studied casualness about him. Somehow I could picture him with dirty sneakers and a squash racket, coming out of the Harvard Club and sliding into an XKE.

"We're just staying here temporarily," he said, glancing around and crossing his legs. "Place is owned by my brother Bill and his wife; they're out on the Island today."

"Oh, I see."

"We're still looking for an apartment. I had no idea it would be so hard. Still have all our furniture in storage. In Detroit. Are you a native New Yorker?"

"Yes, sir, I was born here."

"Where do you live?"

"West End Avenue at Seventy-ninth Street."

"Oh, yes, I've seen that area, very nice. We've looked around there, too. I'm just—the rents seem more reasonable there, too. I'm just—to be honest about it, I'm just a little afraid of the West side. I mean, because of Susan and Polly, you know?"

"Oh, sure."

"I mean, it's bad enough on the *East* Side, from what I hear. All the crime, the muggings."

"Right."

"Anyway, we're still looking, we've got a pretty good agency looking for us. Bill is looking for us, too—Bill and Eunice. But I can't look at places during the day, I'm working. And the girls are in school—Polly's in graduate school up at Columbia."

"I see."

He smiled. "Got any hot tips on apartments?"

"No, sir, I wish I did."

"What's your father do, Jeremy?"

"He's with International Airways. He's assistant vice-president of advertising and sales promotion."

"That's one of my favorite airlines. How long has he been with them?"

"About twenty-two years, I think."

"Long time." He took a drag on the cigarette, sat back, blew smoke at the ceiling. "I once considered going in the airline business. Seems like a long time ago. I probably should've done it."

"Where are you working now?"

He glanced at me just a little sharply. "I'm on Wall Street. Right now I'm a consultant for a brokerage firm—

Parkinson. I'm a stockbroker by trade." He laughed quietly then, as if to himself, glanced at the ceiling. "At least, I *was* a stockbroker before we hit this town. Firm named Wellington Bryant in Detroit. Ever heard of it?"

I was just about to answer no, when a girl walked into the room and we both stood up.

"Oh, here's Polly," he said. "You haven't met her."

Susan's sister walked over to me, smiling, holding an empty coffee cup and saucer. I could see a facial resemblance to Susan, but Polly was blonde, slightly taller and in her early twenties. She wore a dark sweatshirt and jeans, no shoes.

"Hi, Jeremy, how you doing?" She shook my hand with a firm grip. "I spoke to you on the phone this morning."

"Oh, yeah, hi."

"Listen, sit down, I'm just passing through for some more coffee. I'm writing a paper you know? Excuse my appearance."

"Where's Susan?" he asked.

She shrugged. "In her room, I guess. Does she know he's here?"

"I called to her when I rang the buzzer."

"She'll be out." She smiled at me. "Nice meeting you, Jeremy."

"Nice meeting you."

She padded out to the kitchen and we sat down again. Mr. Rollins glanced at his watch. There was a rather long pause.

"Well, I hope you find an apartment," I said, finally.

He nodded, took a last drag on the cigarette and stubbed it out in the ashtray. "It's a tough town you have here."

"I know."

"I thought Detroit was tough, that's why we came here. I thought Wellington Bryant was tough. God, that was *tame,* compared to Wall Street."

Susan came in then, smiling at me. She looked really neat, especially her hair, and she was wearing what was my favorite outfit of hers, the faded blue workshirt with sleeves a little too long—which she wore as a jacket—and the nicely faded, belled Levi's with the ragged bottoms.

"Hi, Jeremy!"

"Hi." I realized that I'd forgotten to stand, and jumped up quickly.

Mr. Rollins looked her up and down, smiling warmly, obviously proud as hell. They seemed to have a special thing between them, glancing at each other.

"You going out on a *date* in that outfit?" he asked, laughing.

"Yeah!"

"My God!" He looked down at the ragged edges of her pants; they touched the floor, covering her feet. "You got any *shoes* on tonight?"

Susan laughed, pushed at him, and he grabbed her and threw his arm around her. Seeing them like that, playing around and happy, I remember revising my first impressions of the man.

"I was just telling Jeremy about our favorite people," he said, hugging her close, facing me. "Wellington Bryant and the Good Guys."

"Oh, God," she groaned.

"Warm-hearted Wellington, huh?"

"May he burn in hell," she said. Then, glancing at me: "I guess we better get going, huh?"

There were probably more W.C. Fields aficionados in New York that year than when he was alive, most of them under thirty and if you had seen the length of the line at the Thalia that evening, you'd have sworn the majority of them were there. It was just incredible. At five forty-five, the ticket-holders' line extended all the way down Broadway, around the corner of Ninety-fourth Street and clear to the middle of that block. I remember a lot of the kids were sitting cross-legged on the sidewalk; they'd been there a long time. I should've anticipated it and I felt embarrassed. Anyway, I waited in the short line to buy tickets then we walked around the corner, all the way to the end.

Standing in line at least gave me the chance to see Susan close up for a while. She looked absolutely great. After five minutes, I saw that the line wasn't moving at all and I knew it wouldn't until six. Those things never started time.

"Gee, I'm sorry," I told her.

"It's okay."

"I never expected this. Y'know, we could be waiting here all night."

"I don't mind waiting."

I looked up toward Broadway, saw the red neon sign of a pizza parlor. "Say, I got an idea. Do you like pizza?"

"Uh-huh."

"I love pizza too. We could go get some instead of waiting in line."

She smiled. "Okay."

I've often wondered what would have happened if we hadn't changed our minds about the movie. I just shoved the tickets in my pocket and we walked up to Broadway, crossed the street and went into the pizza place. It wasn't very large, but it looked clean, with a long counter to the left and two rows of booths to the right. The jukebox was playing rock. Only a few couples were in the booths. The pizza smelled very good. We went up to the counter and the pizza man looked up from his newspaper.

"Hi, how are you?"

"We're okay," I told him.

"What kind of pizza would you like?"

"Plain." I glanced at Susan; she nodded. "A large one, please."

"Sure. Would you like to have a seat?"

We went to a booth away from the other couples and sat facing each other for the first time. She pushed back her hair and glanced around. I decided to continue my strategy of asking questions, at least until I could feel more relaxed.

"Hey, Susan, let me ask you something. What if I hadn't been sent out to get a piece of chalk that day? I probably would never have met you. Do you believe in things like that?"

"Like what?"

"I don't know, like fate."

"Oh, I don't know if I do. I think I'm too practical."

"I believe in those kind of things."

I seem to remember that we went on like that for an eternity, until our pizza was served. I felt painfully awkward, to the point where I couldn't look her in the eyes. I was never so glad to see a pizza in my life. And I'm certain she felt the same.

"Umm," she said. "Looks good. Could I have a Coke, please?"

I caught the man before he left. "Oh, when you get a chance, could you bring us some Cokes?"

"Sure."

"Thanks." I took a slice immediately, but it was too hot to hold. I licked my finger. "That's good."

Susan waited before trying it. "Jeremy, what are you?"

I knew it was coming, but I hesitated. "Sophomore."

She shook her head. "No, I know that. I meant what nationality."

"You knew I was a sophomore?"

"Yeah. Did you think I wouldn't go out with you if I knew?"

"I don't know."

"Things like that don't matter to me."

"Yeah, they don't matter to me, either." I started to eat. The pizza man served our Cokes.

Susan thanked him, then looked me in the eyes. "So what are you, I mean what nationality?"

"Jewish."

"Really?" She seemed surprised.

"Yeah."

"Is Jones your real name?"

"Yeah. Want to know how it happened?"

"Yeah." She picked up a slice, started eating.

"My grandfather's name was Jonas Rochman. When he came to this country from Austria, they were asking for names. And Jonas, he thought he was supposed to say his last name first and his first name last. So he said, 'Rochman, Jonas.' See? Somewhere along the line, Jonas became Jones, and that's it."

She nodded, then frowned. "Hey, are you making this up?"

"No, really. So I guess I'm really Jeremy Rochman."

"Rochman," she said slowly. "I guess I'll call you Rock."

"Oh, no, don't call me Rock . . ."

"I always wanted to call someone Rock."

"No . . ."

"I won't. I'm only kidding."

I smiled with relief. "What are you?"

"Oh, I'm half . . . half French-Canadian, Half Scottish, English, Welsh and Irish."

"Wow. Wow, I like that!"

She paused, watching me. "You know what I like?"

"What?"

"When I heard you playing the cello, I couldn't believe it, you were so good."

"Yeah, well, I guess I really feel things when I play music."

Her voice softened then. "Yeah, I know."

We never did get to that movie. I remember we stayed in the booth and talked for quite a while, over more Cokes, then we decided to take a cab up to the Metropolitan Museum of Art, which was within walking distance of her home, so we could sit by the fountains and talk.

The whole front of the Metropolitan had been redone and it looked fantastic at night with the floodlights on it. There was a huge new staircase, flanked on both sides by long rows of low, graceful fountains falling into shallow pools. Underwater lights played on the fountains as they sprayed. We sat on the edge of one of the long pools and talked, watching people stroll past on Fifth.

"Are you going to be a dancer?" I asked.

"Uh-huh. I hope so."

"I'd like to go to Juilliard. Have you ever heard of that school?"

"Oh, sure." She reached in the pool quickly, threw some water on me. "We did know *some* things in Detroit, y'know!"

I laughed, brushed myself off. "Okay, okay!"

"God, you New Yorkers really knock me out sometimes."

"Well, you can consider yourself a New Yorker now."

"Yeah, one of the elite, huh?"

"Why'd you move here?"

"My dad had to come because of a job." She glanced down at the pool, dipped her hand in it. "He got sort of a rough deal in Detroit. He's not making much headway here, either."

"Are you sorry you left Detroit?"

"No, I don't think so."

"It must have been real hard for you, leaving all your friends."

She shook her head decisively. "Oh, no, I didn't have that many."

"I'm the same way. I don't have many friends, either."

It started to get chilly sitting there, so we walked down Fifth to Seventy-fourth, talking all the time, really finding out about each other. I wanted to learn everything I could about her all at once, but I tried to play it cool. Her street was narrow and tree-lined and had those long rows of proud old four- and five-story brownstones that had once been townhouses. Most had been turned into apartments, but with the high windows and ceilings, thick walls and working fireplaces that I loved.

Her place didn't have a front stoop, so we sat on one a

few doors away, at 34. I kept asking her questions and she didn't seem to mind. She told me a lot about her family.

"So, anyway, my mother died when I was five," she said very softly. "And I lived with my father and different relatives who came over to help, you know?"

"Wow. That must have been rough."

"No, not really. Later on it was really a problem, though." She sat forward, hugging her knees. "I'm not used to talking about myself this much."

"Well, I'd like to hear about it. Unless you just don't want to talk about it, you know?"

"No, that's okay. This is just about it, though. I guess that's why I find it hard to make friends. I'm sort of unsure of myself, I think. I don't know who I am. It's like . . . it's like I'm half a person."

"You don't remember your mother at all?"

"No. Not really. Only from pictures. Some day I'll find out who I am. Do you know who you are?"

I thought about it. "Sometimes."

"When?"

I tried to find the words, but it was difficult, as usual. "I don't know. I know who I'd like to be. I'd like to be a great musician. Music is the only time I feel like I'm me, you know? Not like my parents' little boy or some kid going to school. I mean I feel like a whole person. You understand?"

"Sure." She was staring at me.

"I mean, it like brings the me, you know, the me inside of me, coming out. That doesn't make too much sense. I don't know . . ."

We didn't talk for a while. It was cool and pleasant. The dim streetlights made yellow patterns on the bare branches of the trees and along the cracked sidewalk and you could see other people sitting on stoops down the block and hear their voices sometimes. Couples passed by and an occasional car. An older man walked past with a little Yorkshire terrier on a leash. Susan knew the man and said hello; she ran down quickly and got down on her knees and played with the dog. There was that moist, sharp smell New York has on long autumn nights—before the garbage men come, or the street cleaners—with the trash cans full and overflowing by the curbs, and the feel of soot on the cool, well-worn steps.

Susan came back smiling, tossing the hair away from her face. She sat on the step below me, stretched out, leaning against the wrought-iron railing. Her voice was soft.

"You're funny," she told me.

"Why?"

"When I first met you . . . oh, forget it."

"Tell me. What?"

"Well, you were kinda goofy. And I usually like serious people."

I waited, choosing my words. "Why'd you go out with me?"

She seemed to consider it carefully. "Well, after your concert, I just knew that anybody who could play like that was someone special. I guess that's fate."

I gave her a long look. "Hey, I thought you didn't believe in fate."

"Did I say that?"

I touched her gently under the chin. "Yeah."

"Oh, I *couldn't* of said that." She stood up smiling. "Come on. It's getting cold."

I put my arm around her and we walked a few doors

down to her apartment. I remember how she pressed against me.

"I hope you had fun," I said quietly.

"Oh, yeah . . . thank you."

"Don't say thanks. Come on. Okay? I mean, I didn't do anything."

"Yes, you did."

"What did I do?"

We turned in and stood in front of her doorway. I honestly didn't expect to kiss her good-night, but she put her hands on my shoulders as she answered so easily.

"You made me happy tonight."

I kissed her very softly.

She looked up at me. "Tonight was beautiful."

"You know what's beautiful? You're beautiful."

She was leaning against me then, hands still on my shoulders, face upturned and close. What the hell am I doing, I thought, leaning down and kissing her harder. Then again and again, as if I couldn't get enough of her, which I couldn't. I don't even know how long we were at it. I didn't care.

It was around ten thirty when I got home. Dad was watching a football special on television, highlights of last week's Colts-Vikings game. Mother had already gone to bed. The living room was fairly dark and Dad was sitting at the end of the couch, illuminated by the picture. He looked over at me, squinting.

"Well, how'd it go?" he asked.

"Oh, fine."

"How was the movie?"

"Oh, we didn't go to the movie, we went and had a pizza instead. The line was too long."

He looked at his watch. "You had a pizza all this time?"

"No, I mean we talked and all."

"Uh-huh. You have fun?"

"Oh, yeah, it was great."

"Okay, look, it's late, huh? Tell me about it in the morning. I want to hear all about it, your mother, too."

"Okay. Good-night, Dad."

"Good-night. Glad you had fun."

I knew Ralph would be up and I couldn't wait to tell him. I went into my room, closed the door quietly, sat on the floor and called him. I was bursting to share it with somebody. Ralph's father answered and shouted to him. I could hear their television blaring; they were watching the football special, too. Ralph took the call in the kitchen, where he always talked, and his father hung up the other phone. I think Ralph was trying to listen to me and the game at the same time, because he wasn't getting half what I was saying.

"Ralphy, I couldn't believe I said it. I mean, it's like someone else was in my head saying those words."

"Wait . . . wait . . . tell me again. You said *what*?"

"I told her she was beautiful."

"Oh, my God!" I heard him open the refrigerator, then slam the door.

"Ralphy, it just popped out." I listened to him munching on something, unable to answer. "What am I telling you for anyway?" He continued to munch. "I can't believe I said it."

"Yeah, she probably figured you were a lovesick idiot."

"You want to know something? I'm out of my mind in love."

"I knew this was gonna happen. I knew it."

"Ralphy, I swear to God . . . it's like everything I've ever read. My head's like spinning around. I'm just in love."

"Het, answer me one thing." He made a nasal laughing sound. "You get anything?"

I should've expected it, but it just annoyed me. "Hey, forget it. I can't talk to you. You got no feelings."

"Got no feelings? I was inside watching the Colts and Vikings play. You call me up and tell me you told some girl she was beautiful. What am I supposed to say?"

"Forget it."

"Hey, Jeremy, listen. I really think it's wonderful that you and Susan have found such blissful happiness together. God bless youse both."

The next morning I got up about six o'clock, showered, had a quick bowl of cereal and left the apartment about six thirty, before my parents were even awake. I jogged over to Central Park West, then through the park, just before sunrise, in that unreal first light, and the air smelled of wet leaves. The tops of the buildings surrounding the park were dark walls reaching for the autumn sky, only a few windows lighted, high yellow slits in the night. When I came out on Fifth Avenue, the street was black and wet, already sprinkled with headlights, manholes and sewers steaming, isolated people walking quickly, leaning against the wind.

On Seventy-fourth Street, all the streetlights had misty halos and sometimes you could see leaves blowing into the circles and then vanishing. I passed Susan's apartment about seven o'clock, walking on the opposite side, concealed myself behind one of the stoops not too far away, and waited. The front of the townhouse began to take color about seven thirty and the streetlights went out shortly after that. A large white sanitation truck went past about seven forty-five, spraying both sides of the street simultaneously, leaving blurred reflections of the parked cars, and Susan came out just after that, books in hand.

She walked in the opposite direction, toward Madison, as I thought she would, because she had to catch the downtown bus at Fifth. I sprinted around the block—over to Park, down to Seventy-third, across to Madison, up to Seventy-fourth again—and got there just in time. I was out of breath and had a pain in my side, but seeing her face in the early morning like that was worth it. And her voice, excited at first.

"Jeremy? Hi!"

"Hi, Susan. What are *you* doing here?"

"What am *I* doing here? This is where I live. What're *you* doing here?"

Somehow, I hadn't prepared an answer for that obvious question, so I had to wing it. "Oh . . . I was just on my way to pick up some music supplies. There's a very good music store around here."

"Oh, really? Where? I didn't know that."

I pointed stupidly toward Fifth. "Uh, just up the block somewhere."

"I didn't know there were any music stores around here."

"Sure there are. Umm, between the delicatessen and the drugstore."

She paused. "Wait a minute. There aren't any delicatessens around here, either."

"Sure there are. Ryan's. Ryan's."

"Ryan's?"

I knew damn well I was in too deep, I had to stop. I recall looking down at my sneakers, scuffing one on the pavement, wondering how she'd react to the simple dumb truth. "I'm not very good at this. But I didn't go to any music store. I just wanted to walk you to school, so I came by early and waited for you."

Her voice went soft. "How long have you been waiting?"

"Since seven."

"Really?"

"Yeah." I still couldn't look up at her. "I guess that's kind of dumb, huh?"

"No, it isn't." She tilted her head sideways, leaned in, and kissed me hard on the mouth; when I lifted my chin she opened her mouth slightly and rubbed her lips back and forth against mine, roughly, before drawing back. "That's a good-morning kiss."

I was aware that my hands and legs were trembling. "I never kissed anyone good-morning before."

She took my arm. "Come on."

We began walking, arm in arm.

"You waited all this time?" she asked. "You really waited since seven?"

"Yeah."

We took the bus down Fifth to Forty-sixth Street, then walked west, crosstown, to school. I was excited every minute of the time and I think she enjoyed it too. She was smiling and her face had color. Just being with her like that was sort of unreal to me, watching her eyes, talking with her, listening to her quiet voice. Her eyes and mouth

61

were incredibly expressive, revealing the most subtle variations in mood. At that age, she was miles ahead of me, of course, and I was painfully aware of the difference. Not that she took advantage of it that much, but if she had wanted to manipulate me for an ego trip or whatever, I wouldn't have cared at that stage. I simply couldn't get enough of her, on any terms. I felt on a continual high around her. Occasionally, she'd look at me out of the corner of her eye, or move the corners of her mouth in a certain way, and I knew damn well that she was seeing right through me, but it was all right, it was fine. There were times that morning when I just stared at her openly, like on the bus, when we had to stand all the way: I simply couldn't help staring at her profile, at her clear complexion, and I'm certain she was aware of it as she looked out the window, pushing back her hair, but she handled it so easily. Walking down Forty-sixth Street, my hands and legs were trembling all the time, but she couldn't see my legs and I tried to keep my hands shoved in my pockets. If she noticed, her eyes didn't say anything.

After school, we made the trip in reverse. I couldn't stay with her because I had to walk the dogs. I asked if I could pick her up the next morning, same time, and she answered by giving me a "good-afternoon" kiss, the same lingering way.

I don't even remember walking the dogs that afternoon, but I recall going over to Ralph's afterward, up on West Eighty-sixth Street. We played some one-on-one basketball at a hoop he had in the alley of his apartment building. When we got tired, we had Cokes in his kitchen and talked.

"You know what I like best about her?" I said. "It's the little things."

Ralph leaned back, sipped his Coke, glanced at the ceiling.

"Like the way she says 'hello.'"

He looked at me. "What?"

"Boy, when she says 'hello,' it's so beautiful."

He nodded and leaned forward. "I don't like what's happening to you at all, man."

"Ralphy, it's so beautiful."

"I've heard her say 'hello' before. Plenty of times. Never hit me as anything special."

"Depends on how she says it."

"How does she say it?"

"It's not that important."

"It *is* important." He put down his Coke. "I want to know how she says it."

I paused, trying to remember exactly. "All right. Look, it—this isn't exactly it. It goes something like this. Uh, like . . . you're not listening."

"Yeah, come on."

"Okay, now it's—the way she says it—it's like . . ." I pursed my lips and started to speak very quietly. "Her voice is all low . . . quiet . . . ready? 'Hello.'"

He waited, as if expecting more. "'Hello.' That's it?"

"Yeah, that's it."

He shook his head, stared into space. "I swear . . . they're going to take you away. I *know* they're going to take you away."

"You know what it's called?"

"What?"

63

"It's called *love*."

"You know what that's called? *Dumb*."

I picked Susan up every morning that week, but rather than jog through the park (which got me kind of sweaty that first time), I started taking the crosstown bus. We had lunch dates in the cafeteria every day and I began looking forward to that hour so much that I could hardly stand it in class. I started writing her name on the covers of my notebooks then and drawing pictures of her on the pages. We met in the corridors after certain classes, when they weren't too far apart; this resulted in my being slightly late for two classes that week, but I managed to con my way out of trouble both times. After school every day, we walked together and then took the bus back to her apartment, but I could never stay because of my job. I began to hate that job, despite my love for the dogs, but I knew I couldn't just quit; my father would've killed me.

I remember looking forward to our first whole weekend together. Thursday afternoon I called Max and arranged to have my Saturday morning music lesson at eleven rather than ten, because I had something special planned. When I met Susan Friday morning, I decided to keep it sort of a secret.

"I'll pick you up early Saturday morning," I told her.

"How early?"

"Six a.m."

"Six a.m.?"

"Yup, six o'clock in the morning."

She moved the corner of her mouth in that special way. "Ummm, yeah, I suppose so. What for?"

"It's a surprise."

She smiled and didn't say anything for a while. "Well, okay. Call me before you're ready to leave and make sure I'm up."

"Yeah, I'll call. But you've got to be ready at six."

5

She was leaning against the wall in the lighted lobby of her building when I arrived just a few minutes before six, but when I tapped on the glass of the inside door, she pretended to be asleep in that position: head limp to one side, hair covering her face, arms by her sides. She looked so neat like that, I had to laugh out loud. When she heard me, her shoulders started to shake, then her head, then she was laughing openly, pretending to be sleepwalking, arms out in front groping, hair still over her face. Trying to control her laughter, she opened the door like a robot, reached out, touched my face, explored it with feverish excitement, finally wedged her fingers in my nostrils.

"Oh, Elvis," she said dreamily. "You've finally come for me!"

I answered in a rather nasal drawl. "Didn't bring my guitar, though. Too freakin' *heavy*."

Outside, it was dark and cold and the street was deserted. We walked east toward the Lexington Avenue subway, huddled together.

"Six o'clock in the morning," she said, teeth chattering. "I can't believe it. Won't you tell me where we're going?"

"Nope."

"Come on, just a little hint?"

"No."

She nudged me. "Come on."

"All right. One hint. That's it, all right?"

"Okay."

I stopped and faced her. "Okay, you ready?" I held one hand above the other, snapped the fingers of one hand, then the other, then pounded my fist into my palm. Next time I accelerated the three steps, increasing the tempo each subsequent time. until I was producing that peculiar rhythm—*snap-snap-pound, snap-snap-pound, snap-snap-pound*—that I'd learned several years before. Susan looked absolutely puzzled, but to me it sounded exactly like the hoofbeats of a galloping horse.

At Grand Central, we changed over to the Independent line, got an E train out to Parsons Boulevard in Queens and arrived at Belmont Park just before seven o'clock.

We walked to the south entrance near Hempstead Avenue, because I wanted Susan to see the huge paddock area first. Even in cool autumn dawn, the wide lawn and sculptured shrubbery were green and lush and fresh-smelling, and the family of four white ducks were long awake then, circling the big pond, scattered with leaves, soft ripples bending clear reflections of the bare tree branches. After the subway, it was like suddenly stepping into calm countryside. We could even hear birds chirping.

We went into the grandstand and down one of the aisles. The long, modern, triple-decked stands threw a deep shadow across the wide blacktop area below, so that you could barely see the rows of unpainted benches, and the shadow spilled onto the track itself, then became lost in low fog from the infield lagoon. But as you walked closer to the rail, you could see the horses clearly and hear them and smell them. In those first few minutes, I found myself sort of reappraising various things in terms of how excited Susan was about them. Seeing the horses themselves really seemed to knock her out. I remember her eyes when the first one galloped past, fairly close to the rail.

"Oh, look at him!" she said.

"Wow. Look at that stride."

"He's *beautiful*."

"Yeah. Now you know why they call it 'breezing.' "

"Yeah . . . it's that they run so smooth. Sort of breeze by."

Another one came close, gliding past, with the jockey standing up in the saddle.

"Yeah, it's kind of like music," I told her.

"Do they train like this every morning?"

"Yeah. They start out here about dawn. Look at 'em go."

A horse thundered past, extremely close, and I watched Susan's eyes all the time.

"Jeremy, when you said we were going someplace special, I never thought we'd wind up here."

I hesitated. "Don't you like it?"

"Oh, I love it!"

"Great."

"It's just sort of weird seeing you at a race track."

69

"Is that okay?"

"Oh, God, it's fantastic!"

"Oh, great," I said, watching her eyes. "You know, I used to spend every summer here. Well, about two or three years ago, for three years in a row. Yeah, I used to do like a hot-walker for my uncle. I used to—yeah, I used to feed the horses and walk 'em. That's what a hot-walker does. It was so nice."

She hugged me. "Oh, Jeremy, you amaze me."

"You know, it's funny, my dad used to be the same as me when he was a kid. He loved horses, he did the same job I used to do."

"Yeah?"

"Yeah. But now—now he doesn't have time for that kind of stuff. He's too busy. Come on, I'll show you Bill Wingate's barn." I put my arm around her and we started toward the exit. "He used to be a really good friend of my dad's."

It took us about ten minutes to walk all the way over to the Wingate stable. Ordinarily, the public isn't allowed inside, but I knew the security guy, Jim Turner, who had been one of my friends during the summers I worked there, and he let us through right away. As Susan smiled and went past, I saw him check her out with that quick glance he had. You should've seen the look he gave me.

That stable really brought back happy memories. It was very long and rather dark, open at both ends, with dozens of individual stalls on one side. Most of the horses' heads were sticking out of their stalls, as usual, and I remember the smell particularly—a cool, damp combination of hay, manure and leather. In the summer, it was one of the coolest spots at the track; the smell was much stronger then and—if you loved horses—very pleasant. As we walked past the stalls, I started to tell Susan about my favorite horse, Sinbad.

"He's a gray gelding," I said, excited to be sharing it with her. "He's really fantastic." Then I saw him, his head sticking out about three stalls down, his eye looking at us. "Oh, here he is. This is Sinbad."

We went up to him and I patted him on the head and took a good look at his body. He was even more beautiful than I'd remembered: steel gray and sleek as hell, with tremendous conformation, and unusually broad in the brisket—the breast—which made him long on wind.

I remember Susan going, "Oooh."

"Yeah, his sire was Never Bend, out of Ambriarch's mare. Know what that means?"

"No."

"Oh, well, a sire means the father and the mare is the mother."

"Oh." She was staring at him, sort of mesmerized.

"Want to feed him a piece of sugar?"

"Yeah."

I handed her one of the pieces I'd brought from home. "Here."

She held the lump up to his mouth rather gingerly.

I tried to reassure her. "Usually, horses with Nashbula blood are mean, but he's good."

She reached up to pat his head as she fed him, but Sinbad snorted and shook his head at that. She pulled her hand back quickly and laughed. I helped her with the sugar.

71

"Well, look, hold your hand out flat. Here. That's it. See, these horses are inbred and they're really jumpy, but he's okay. Whoops, he dropped it. Here." I picked up the lump and guided her hand to his mouth. Sinbad took it and started munching away. But I don't think he liked her. I could tell by his eyes. "Come on, I'll show you some other horses."

We walked along, arm in arm.

"Do you ever bet on the races?" she asked.

"No, I handicap them for fun, but I never bet."

"Well, why not?"

"Well, I guess I'd rather spend my money on music and records and stuff like that."

"Well, can you give me a good tip?"

"Yeah, sure. Billy Blue in the fourth."

"You're sure he'll win?"

"Absolutely."

After a while, we went back to the track and watched them exercise again and I think Susan liked that a lot better than the stables. The sun came up and it got a little warmer and then eventually most of the horses were taken inside to be groomed. I was satisfied that Susan had seen just about everything I'd wanted her to see, so we left around ten o'clock.

We took the subway in to Brooklyn, changed for Brighton Beach and arrived out there in plenty of time for my music lesson. Susan had never seen that area, so she spent the time exploring the boardwalk and beach. Afterward, we had lunch at one of the hot-dog stands before taking the subway back.

I remember we sat on the steps of a brownstone near

her house and I decided to entertain her by going through my racing-announcer bit. I could imitate racetrack announcers pretty well by then. I had already bought *The Racing Form* and handicapped all the races, so I decided to call the more exciting ones, inventing all the action:

"That's Triple Ben still in the lead. Two lengths and Famous City and Aplomb second and third, with Peace Corps following far behind. As they come into the stretch, that's Triple Ben and Tunix . . . that's Triple Ben and Tunix . . . Triple Ben and Tunix. As they cross the wire, it's—Triple Ben!"

Susan was laughing softly, half enjoying it and half embarrassed. "Does anybody else know you do this?"

"Nope. It's a secret."

"Good." She glanced away, then gave me that look from the corner of her eye. "I wouldn't tell 'em if I were you."

"Okay. You know what else I do?"

"What?"

"Promise you won't laugh? It's kind of stupid."

"I promise."

"Well, sometimes when I'm walking down the street, I see some guy ahead of me—you know, just any guy—I want to race him. You know, just me and him, and I create an imaginary finish line. I call the race in my head."

Susan bit her lip, glanced up at the sky. "I don't believe it." She looked at me with that intuitive gaze that made me feel much younger than she was—mentally, physically, emotionally. It was a gaze that I could always feel in my stomach.

I can't be certain, but I suspect that I *wanted* to feel

73

that way. I wanted her to have that edge. I wanted her to make me bleed. I wanted her to hurt me and know it and feel a responsibility for having done that. I wanted to tell her some of my stupid secrets that I'd never, ever, told anyone else, things that embarrassed me more than they did her, because I wanted her to understand exactly how far ahead she really was. It's difficult to explain an emotion like that, even now. She was so beautiful to me—so brilliant, so talented—that I felt deeply inferior by comparison: ugly, awkward, unsophisticated. I think I loved her so much that I worshiped her. Any given move she made could arouse me instantly. I don't mean gradually, I mean instantly. Almost every time I was with her, my hands and legs would continue to tremble, no matter how casual my posture, no matter how successful I was at controlling my voice. I would have done virtually anything she asked me to do, even beyond reasonable limits because I was thinking with my emotions.

So, conjuring up an image in my mind of one of the countless "races" I'd run against unsuspecting people on the street, I called the race out loud in my best announcer's voice. "And they're off! The man in the blue suit has a two-length lead as they come out of the starting gate, and Jeremy Jones is a disappointing second. On the outside, Jones makes his move. At the sixteenth pole, it's Jones and the man in the blue suit, neck and neck. As they come down the home stretch, blue suit is ahead . . . the man in the blue suit and Jeremy Jones . . . the man in the blue suit and Jeremy Jones . . . the man in the blue suit and Jeremy Jones. As they cross the wire, it's— *Jeremy Jones!*"

Her face had colored slightly, and she was looking away. Her hair covered most of her profile.

"Hey," I said softly.

"Uh-huh."

"Hey, I'm sorry."

"Don't be."

"Listen, Susan, would you do something for me? I've been—I'd like to have something of yours. Anything, as long as it's something personal, you know? Something that you like. That I could, like, carry around in my pocket, you know?"

She looked at me then, first out of the corner of the eye.

"Is that okay?" I asked.

She faced me, the corners of her mouth smiling. "Sure. What kind of thing?"

"I don't know. Just something of yours that I could keep. I mean, I'll give you something of mine too . . . if you want."

"What, your basketball?"

"No, come on, really."

She laughed softly, nodded, glanced at the gold signet ring on the middle finger of her right hand. It was her "Rio" ring, the one her father bought her in Rio de Janeiro on their one big trip together, the previous year. She was never without it.

"No, I don't want that," I told her. "It's too good, you like it too much."

She turned the ring on her finger, her hair falling forward.

"I don't want it, Susan, really."

"Okay. I'll think of something."

75

"Just something simple, without much value. That you like."

She tossed her hair back, smiled. "What're you going to give me?"

"Well, like I've been thinking about it, you know? The thing is, I don't have a lot of little things. Like jewelry and things like that. I mean I just have a few."

"Uh-huh." She smiled with the corners of her mouth again, as if she knew exactly what I was going to say.

"Well, there's this really neat Indian store down on Second Avenue, down in the Forties, they sell authentic American Indian stuff. So last summer I was in there, looking around—you should see the stuff they have—and I bought something on the spot, I liked it so much."

"Uh-huh," she said very softly. "A shrunken head, huh?"

I burst out laughing, then felt suddenly stupid about the whole thing. I'd rehearsed the presentation too, and I'd been looking forward to it. I think she understood, because she made a determined effort to stop laughing and look serious again.

"Oh, man, come on," I said.

"Okay."

"Okay? Because it's—"

"Okay, okay, I'm sor—" She broke up laughing then, so much so that her eyes started to water.

When she was all right again, wiping her eyes, I reached in my jacket pocket and brought out the strand of colored beads, along with two lumps of sugar that were left over. It was a small, rather delicate strand of red and blue beads, handmade, that I'd actually bought for her several days before.

"Oh, Jeremy."

"Yeah, I thought you'd like it."

"Oh, it's—beautiful!"

She leaned forward as I placed the strand over her head. I remember her face as she adjusted it under her hair. I kissed her on the lips, but I did it very awkwardly, not the way I had planned.

6

When I woke up Sunday morning, my ceiling was bathed in a soft flickering light and I knew it was raining. That excited me, because it gave me the excuse I'd been trying to find. Mother and Dad were going to spend the day with friends and the apartment would be empty from noon until about six, or perhaps even longer if they decided to have dinner out. Susan had wanted to see a movie that afternoon, but I remember I wasn't quite sure I wanted to do that, for a very selfish reason. If we went to a movie, I wouldn't really be able to look at her or talk with her for a whole two hours of our afternoon, or however long the film took, and I thought of it somehow as wasted time. Of course, the idea *had* crossed my mind that if the theater wasn't too crowded and we sat way back in the balcony or something, we could neck through the whole flick, or at least part of it, but I'd never done that and I suspected that Susan might not go for it anyway. The rain gave me a perfect excuse to change plans. I called her up about nine o'clock and invited her over to play chess. We had never played each other, but we both liked the game, and she seemed enthusiastic about the idea.

I went over to pick her up just after my parents left, about noon, then splurged on a taxi back to the apartment, but we were still pretty wet when we arrived. It was really coming down. I showed her through the apartment and it was exciting to see her reactions.

We played chess on the floor of my room. As I expected, she was much better at it than I was, but I didn't really care. Having her alone in my room like that was all I wanted. I remember I wasn't concentrating at all. I placed my Bishop in line with her Queen, which was in the last rank.

"Sure you want to do that?" she asked quietly.

"Yeah, sure."

"Okay." She took my Bishop with her Queen.

"Susan, let me ask you something. We've been going out together for a while now." I paused, trying to get the words right. "Well, have you been having fun?"

"Yeah, haven't you?"

"Oh, yeah. Yeah, of course. That's not what I meant. What I mean is—uh—well, I'm kind of serious, you know. I mean, basically I'm kind of a serious person. I guess I'm kind of quiet. I was just wondering if you were having a good time."

She frowned. "Jeremy, sometimes I don't understand you. I mean, do you really feel you have to ask me that?"

"I mean I really like spending the afternoon here with you. Talking . . . looking out at the rain . . . playing chess. I know it's not too exciting. If you'd rather go someplace else, we can go."

"Jeremy, you don't have to take me places. I mean, that's not what a relationship is all about."

"You really feel that way?"

"Yes, I feel that way. Of course I feel that way. I mean, spending the day together . . . talking . . . it's great."

"I'm glad." I'd been sitting cross-legged and I shifted to my side, braced by my elbow. I tried to think of a way to word the question I had to ask. "Let me ask you something else. Remember that guy you used to go out with?"

"Danny?"

"Yeah. Well, I don't mean to start anything, but . . . I thought you said you weren't going to see him any more."

"I . . . I haven't seen him since I started going out with you."

I hesitated, not knowing exactly how to put it. "Yeah, well, Ralphy said that he saw you with him yesterday . . . after school."

"Oh, that. I just had to speak to him."

"Did you tell him you weren't going to see him any more?"

"I told him something much better than that."

"What?"

I remember she looked down at the floor. When she answered, it was almost in a whisper. "I told him that I loved you."

It surprised me so much that I could hardly believe she said it. "Did you really tell him that?"

She lifted her head then and looked straight in my eyes. "I really told him that."

"Do you really love me?"

"Yeah," she said quietly. "Is that okay?"

"Is that *okay*? God, yeah! I mean, like I feel the same way about you." I paused, reaching for the words. "It's just that I can't say it yet."

She shook her head slowly. "You don't have to say it. Just so long as I know that's how you feel."

"That's how I feel."

We stared at each other, both smiling warmly with that new understanding, and I remember she made a low sound in her throat as I moved toward her, and tossed her hair back with that familiar motion of the head. I was about to say something when she placed her hands behind my neck and kissed me very hard on the mouth, rubbing her lips from side to side. Then we were on the floor so easily and she was very exciting and very good in a smooth, unhurried way, playing, laughing, no hangups at all. But when we realized it was going to be more than that, much more, we were somehow awkward and shy with one another, perhaps even frightened, knowing that the first experience could not be easy, could not be forgotten, could not be taken back and could never conceivably be equal to the fantasies of imagination.

Somehow, we made the first time last. I found that wasn't easy for me, it was extremely difficult, I was all over her, I thought I couldn't possibly wait. But I waited. And we said all the things, and meant them, and lost ourselves in the present moment, getting everything out of it we could get. I remember the feel of her skin and her hair going all over me and the quick, supple way she moved around, trying anything that came to mind, as if it were a game, laughing, experimenting, watching my reactions. And how I felt. And how she looked when it was over. And how strangely proud I was for both of us.

In the late afternoon, when we took a taxi back to her apartment, it was still raining. The traffic lights threw red and green drops on the windshield and the wipers blurred the colors back and forth. We were quiet for most of the ride. I recall Susan sitting back, looking out the window, the headlights of passing cars moving across her face.

"What are you thinking about?" I asked, finally.

"Nothing, really."

"Is there anything wrong?"

"No." She looked at me. "I'm just—wispy."

"Wispy? What's that?"

"I don't know. Happy. Kind of quiet. Something like that."

"Are you happy?"

"Yes." She smiled with the corners. "Are you?"

"Yeah." I thought about it. "Kind of—wispy."

She laughed, pushed at me. "Don't make fun."

When we arrived, she explained that I couldn't go up because her father had guests. That was fine; I didn't want to go up. We stood by the outside door for a while, just under the little convex roof supported by the pillars. The rain had changed gradually to a light but steady drizzle and the air was fresh and smelled of leaves. Susan was leaning against the door, fidgeting with her "Rio" ring.

"I haven't decided what to give you yet," she told me.

"That's all right."

"I have to take my time; it has to be just right."

She looked down at the ring. It was a man's, really,

solid gold and rather heavy. Its flat oval signet held the impression of what was probably some family crest: the image of a castle with three battlement towers and a figure that was half-lion, half-dragon atop the middle tower. There was a very small inscription below the castle, in capital letters almost worn away.

"What's the inscription say again?"

She glanced at it. "Oh, it's—written backwards, you know, for sealing letters and all. It reads 'Perseverando.' —you've seen it."

"Oh, yeah. Persever—?"

"Per-sever-ando. Roughly, it means, 'persevere.' It represents past, present and future."

"Perseverando," I said, getting it right.

She smiled. "Yeah, see, you persevered. Dad gave it to me as a kind of a—consolation gift in Rio. I picked it out myself in one of the little antique shops in the Copacabana area."

"What do you mean, *consolation* gift?"

"Oh, it was just . . ." She glanced at the rain hitting the tops of the parked cars. "It was just because of something I—we saw. In Rio. And Dad tried to make up for it, somehow, by giving me a gift. He said I could have anything I wanted. To cheer me up, I suppose."

"What happened, what'd you see?"

She nodded, breathed deeply. "Every time there's a strong smell of rain, almost every time, it seems to come back. Can't get it out of my mind somehow. It was my first real trip, our only big trip together. And we—I remember we tried to think of the most fabulous place in the world we could go, that we could afford."

"Rio had to be it."

"God, even the name sounded exciting. We made our hotel reservation months in advance at a hotel right on Copacabana Beach, can't even remember the name of it now, we'd made it *months* in advance. Well, we arrive on the scene, they'd never heard of us—no record, no reservation, *sinto muito pesaroso*. And I mean it wasn't a question of going somewhere else, there *weren't* any other rooms, all the hotels on the beach were booked. God, I can see that lobby now. Standing there at the desk while my father and the room clerk shouted at each other. Bellhops glancing around, embarrassed, and off through the cocktail lounge I could see it raining on the beach and the big breakers coming in."

"Your *fabuloso* holiday."

"My *fabuloso* Rio that I'd dreamed about."

She was silent for a while, leaning back against the door, smiling to herself, remembering. The rain made a soft spattering on the sidewalk and we could hear murmurs of thunder.

"So, anyway, we got the room, finally," she said. "Overlooking the beach, too. The Miramar it was, that's right, sixth floor of the Miramar, our window overlooked Copacabana. It was my spring vacation, the middle of March, the end of the Brazilian summer, always mild and beautiful, right? The ideal time to go, everybody said so, right? Rained almost every day. Absolutely dynamite. I told everybody I'd come back absolutely black, and after a week I was a ghost—and blessed with the squits."

"Oh, no."

"Oh, yeah. Everybody warned me about the water, Dad told me to order *Agua Lindoya,* which I did, but we forgot about the *ice!"*

She laughed softly, turned and met my eyes, then glanced beyond me to the street. Her eyes changed, as if she'd seen something unpleasant.

"What is it?" I asked.

"Nothing, Jeremy, just the rain. Come on, it's getting dark, I'd better go in."

"What is it? Tell me."

She glanced at the street again, frowned, shook her head.

"You want to talk about it?" I asked.

"It's just something that keeps returning, you know? With the smell of rain, it's silly, really. I saw something in Rio that frightened me, that's all. It was just—nothing, really, two days before we were supposed to leave. Friday it was, yeah, the sun came out beautifully in the late afternoon. We'd given up the idea of a tan anyway, so we decided to go see some of the major tourist things, you know, so it wouldn't be a total loss. Well, okay, Sugarloaf, I wanted to go up and see the view from Sugarloaf, but you had to go by cablecar, right? Like a ski-tow across the mountains, then transfer to another cablecar to reach the summit. Well, my stomach wasn't up to that. So we took a taxi up to Corcovado. That's—you know Corcovado?"

"The mountain with the statue?"

"Yeah, the enormous concrete statue of Christ overlooking the city, you can see it for miles in all directions. It's about an hour's drive from Copacabana, up winding mountain roads. So we took a taxi, there was a special rate. About halfway up, the road narrows to just barely two lanes, no guardrails, and the higher you get, the steeper the incline, with the most treacherous curves I've ever seen. Well, our luck continued, it turned out that just about every tourist in town picked that one rare sunny afternoon to see Corcovado, too. I mean, traffic near the top was backed up at least a mile. Cars were stalled and pushed to the sides of the road, you had to wait your turn and maneuver around them, coming and going. We crept along for—I'd say at least two hours, the driver cursing a blue streak in Portuguese; it was a flat round-trip rate, as I said. About five thirty, we got to a small parking area up near the summit, most of the cars seemed to be heading down by that time, and our driver pulled in and motioned for us to walk the rest of the way, that he'd wait. It was almost sundown then and we thought we'd get there too late to take pictures. So we hurried up the turns through the tangled cars, you know, horns blowing, men yelling at each other. Then up the stairs, six or eight levels of stairs to the top, we had to stop and sit a couple of times. Dad wasn't in that great shape. I could smell the rain then. But we went on, we were determined to make it up there before the sun went down. Well, I mean, it was worth it. It really was. From the terrace just below the statue, it's something like twenty-three hundred feet above sea level, with an incredible view of Rio, Sugarloaf, the beaches and bays, everything. All the people were taking pictures, it was getting dark quickly, but I just—I had to sit down on a bench. I don't know what it was, the climb or what, but I couldn't seem to catch my breath."

She crossed her arms over her chest, hugging herself, staring at the street. I waited, but she didn't continue. She seemed lost in her thoughts.

"Then what happened?" I asked quietly.

"I've got to go in, Jeremy."

"First tell me."

"That was all, I just—"

"Please tell me."

She bit her lip, glanced down and away. "It's—difficult to explain. I tried to get some pictures of the statue. It's over a hundred feet tall, absolutely gigantic. Christ the Redeemer, his arms spread wide in a sort of benediction, looking down over the city. The sun was setting behind it, so the face was in deep shadow, the whole front was dark. The sun went down and a while later the floodlights were turned on it. Floodlights surround the statue, the light bouncing off—or seeming to—making it appear luminous, pure white. His face had Brazilian features, with with the eyes staring blankly, almost blindly. I looked at it for a long time, I couldn't help it. Dad did, everybody did. Then you could see the lights of the city starting to come on, far below. You almost felt like whispering, standing there in the darkness below that thing. You could hear dogs barking in the distance. It was a feeling I'll remember all my life."

"What frightened you?" I asked.

"When we were about to start down, I smelled the rain again. That strong smell of like—tropical rain. Well, it started to come down then, within minutes. Not hard, not at first, just a gentle rain, a warm summer shower. Still, everybody ran. There wasn't any cover anywhere around the statue, so we all ran down the stairs to the souvenir stand two levels down. By the time we got there, it was packed. Well, we were pretty well drenched anyway, so Dad decided, the hell with it, we'd walk back in the rain. Traffic was moving finally, it'd thinned a lot on the side going down, in fact that side was moving quickly. All the cars had their headlights on. We walked on a narrow path on the side of the road. Gradually, the rain came harder, much harder, then it was like a real tropical downpour. At one point, I could hardly see. Horns started blowing. I remember being afraid we might be hit, that they couldn't see us. They were going fast on our side, on the outside, and it was too late to cross over. We could hear music from the car radios as they went past, even with their windows closed. Then, at a sharp curve just beyond us, a little car suddenly skidded sideways off the road and went right over the edge. It all happened so fast I—everybody slammed on their brakes, stunned, doors flung open, radios blaring. We heard the first heavy crash of metal and glass over the music, then another more distant splintering, then the sky lit up in a quick red flash an instant before the explosion from below. I remember it echoed like gunfire."

"Okay, don't say any more, Susan, I under—"

"I'd seen the—I'd seen the faces of the people in the car. Just a glimpse as they skidded sideways. Then they were gone. People were screaming and yelling. Everyone was running toward the edge. There were thick black skid marks starting at the white line, wavering, going off the road. The strong smell of gasoline smoke, I remember that, but we couldn't see the smoke. Everyone was shouting and running, it was like they'd all gone crazy. I—ran away down the road, ran away alone. And looked back.

All the cars were parked at crazy angles, motors running, headlights on. All the doors open, radios still playing. A crowd was at the edge, looking over, Dad was with them. Horns started blowing all up and down the mountain. It was crazy. It was like a dream, like the whole world had gone crazy. I was frightened and crying. I looked up and saw the statue, huge and white in the rain."

7

The rest of that night and even Monday morning I was about as close to a state of euphoria as I've ever been in my life. It was like experiencing a continual high, without drugs of any kind. Or, rather, with Susan as the drug: because, in retrospect, I suppose that's about as accurate an explanation for my feelings as I can express in words. After finally kissing her at the door, I walked all the way home and I honestly felt stoned out of my head. There's just no better way to describe it. The few times I'd smoked grass or popped uppers or gotten drunk were relatively poor comparisons. I remember I decided to walk for the specific purpose of enjoying and prolonging the feeling, but the walk itself became something of a blur. The drizzle finally stopped, I recall that, and I remember running up the big stairway of the Metropolitan Museum and then running down again, improvising some wild dance steps, completely oblivious to anyone around. I recall running a great deal, with people and cars and colors blurring; swinging around lampposts and laughing out loud; and even at one point actually running across the tops of a line of cars parked closely along the curb, knowing vaguely, I suppose, that because I was wearing sneakers it was perfectly all right, and that I could outrun any cop who saw me, anyway. That's what I mean by stoned.

I had difficulty sleeping, of course, I thought about Susan just all the time. Her face had the new expressions she'd revealed in my room, the new eyes, the new mouth. My room assumed an entirely new significance because she had been in it. I tried to remember details about our time there, to recall how it felt when she actually admitted she loved me, and the way she looked straight in my eyes and asked, "Is that okay?" I tried to remember exactly how that felt, the sudden punch in your stomach when someone you love says it to you for the first time. And to recall how it felt to discover her whole body for the first time, to touch gently, to know that it was all right to do that and not something to be embarrassed about or ashamed about or to feel guilty about doing. I remember the way she lifted her chin, just perceptibly, in a sort of fierce pride, as if with the intuitive knowledge that our bodies were damn beautiful and should be appreciated by both of us to the fullest, and the hell with anybody who wanted to argue the point.

I went to sleep with those visions, finally, and woke up with them, still high, stoned, looking forward to seeing her so much that I thought I'd go crazy waiting. I suppose if I'd been a bit less naïve, and perhaps several years older, I might have made a conscious effort to come down a little in the cold light of morning, to say to myself: Cool it, Jeremy, just a trifle; because people simply don't go around on a continual high, reality isn't like that, you have to come down sometime, and when you do, it's going to hurt more if you have to fall a long way. But I didn't come down at all, and I knew I was making the mistake again: I was thinking with my emotions. It was a childlike thing to do and stupid and you paid for it dearly. It was a bad mistake and dangerous and I know I was making it again, but I was simply too happy to care. It was like pulling down a shade in the mind.

It was noon before I realized that something was seriously bothering Susan. We were walking down the stairs toward the cafeteria.

"Susan, what's wrong?"

She shook her head. "Jeremy."

Without saying anything else, she led me around the corner and walked ahead, alone, in to the dark auditorium.

"Susan!"

I stood there for a second, then bolted into the auditorium after her. I could hear her stumbling around, searching for the light switch near the door. I began feeling around for it, too, exasperated by all the mystery.

"Where's the light?" I stumbled over something, swore at it, then found the switch and flicked it on roughly.

Susan walked toward a row of seats, avoiding my eyes. I tried to calm down as I followed and sat next to her.

"Susan? What's the matter?"

She wouldn't look at me. "It's so awful."

"What's so awful? Please tell me! Susan?" I reached over, touched her cheek.

"Last night was so beautiful," she said finally, looking at me. "After we kissed, I stood there for a long time. I could still feel your lips on mine. I could still feel you all over my body. And I thought to myself, I'm a woman and he loves me. Then I went inside, I just wanted to be alone, I just wanted to think about you the whole rest of the night. Do you know what I mean?"

"Yeah, I know."

"Then, inside, there were a bunch of people there. And my dad was there." She paused, glanced away. "And he told me we're moving back to Detroit."

"Uh?"

Her voice changed, getting higher. "In two days, we're leaving."

"Detroit?"

"My dad got this new job. We have tickets, I've got to pack."

I nodded dumbly. "When will you be back?"

Her voice went higher. "Jeremy, I'm not coming back, don't you understand?"

"Oh, my God!"

"Jeremy, what're we going to do?" She was crying then, her voice breaking, sounding almost hysterical, and her eyes were pleading. "I've always been so alone . . . I've always felt so outside of things . . . I never had any friends . . . I never had anybody I could be really close to. Oh, Jesus!"

She placed her head on my chest and cried very hard and I think it was only then that my mind began allowing the reality of the thing to be absorbed, although my voice was saying the opposite:

"Look, you can stay in New York. You'll stay with your aunt, and maybe my dad will get your dad a job. You don't have to go."

She couldn't speak.

"What about school?" I asked. "I mean, you can't just—"

"That's all—arranged," she said into my chest, then pushed away. Her face was lovely and angry, streaked with tears, her eyes full. "Mr. Bryant is on the school board, too, and he—"

"Who?"

"—assured my dad that . . . Mr. Bryant, the president of the brokerage, my dad's former firm, the man who hired him back. He assured Dad that I could go back to Jefferson as a junior and not lose any time or credits for the time I missed."

"That's ridiculous! You've been here almost two months now, he can't just—"

"Oh, yes, he can," she said, wiping her face roughly with the palms of her hands, her voice very low then, snapping the words. "He can do anything he wants to do, because he's got *power*. The son of—the son of a bitch, he—steps on people like Dad and forces them to resign and relocate and screw up their lives. Then he offers them the world to come back, because he can't *make* it without them. And they—they come running. He offered —first he apologized for his mistake, they always do that. Then he offered Dad a five-year contract, a twenty percent increase, stock options, the works. And Dad took it, of course he came running."

I was staring at her; I'd never seen her like that before.

"Look, I'll see you this afternoon. I've got to talk with my father."

"About *what*?"

"Just—never mind. See you this afternoon."

I left school immediately and walked in the general direction of my father's office. Then I remembered he had a folk singing commercial they were going to record that Monday. I stopped in a telephone booth on the street, called his office and got the name and address of the recording studio—Reeves, on East Forty-fourth Street, studio five, fourth floor.

Walking crosstown in the noon crowds, I started daydreaming again, as if my mind just flatly refused to deal with this kind of crazy reality. But it was a different kind of fantasy, one that I knew was hallucinatory, because it was based on a vivid dream that seemed to recur whenever I was under particular stress. I had experienced flashes of the dream on the street before, and although it was frightening, sometimes I tried to recall it by stopping quickly and closing my eyes, a trick I used with occasional success. It worked this time, to the extent that I experienced a few major portions of the dream, which I suppose my mind was only too willing to entertain. I didn't close my eyes this time and I didn't even stop walking. The images came anyway:

My bedroom seemed to be invested with shafts of vestigial light and I had an awareness of being in the presence of someone. As usual, my window was open. I went to it and looked out on a vast flat landscape. There was a massive and oppressive sense of weight. It was haunting, something like Dürer's watercolor, *The Deluge*, which I had stared at for so long in Vienna's Kunsthistorisches Museum several years before. I could see an immense, vertical body of water falling *Jeremy I'm not coming back don't you understand* from the sky about four miles from me, descending from such a great height that it seemed to fall *I'm not coming back* very slowly at first, then progressively faster as it approached the earth, roaring with wind, finally striking *I never had anybody I could be really close to* the land with tremendous force and noise, fanning out in tidal waves that swept across miles. Soon, similar *I've always felt so outside of things* bodies of water fell, dozens, like gigantic raindrops, floating down with proportional slowness, increasing *Jeremy what're we going to do* in velocity as they approached, then exploding over the landscape *What're we going to do* with a devastating cumulative effect, an almost apocalyptic—

"Jeremy!" My father's voice was harsh and mechanical, booming from the studio loudspeaker, and I was in reality quickly, whirling around to see him through the long glass window in the control room. I had wandered into studio five at Reeves in the middle of the recording session. The folk singers looked at me blankly, holding their guitars.

My voice, picked up by the studio microphone, also sounded harsh, mechanical, unreal. "Oh, hi, Dad. Dad?

"Yeah?

"Uh, I didn't know where to look for you."

"Sorry, son. Stay there. I'll be right out."

He stood up and walked out of the control room. The technicians in there looked at me strangely. In a moment, Dad came in through the thick studio door and walked silently across the carpet, frowning. I remember the microphone was still on and it made us sound mechanical again.

"How'd you know I was here?"

"Called your office."

"Anything wrong?"

"No. Dad, I've got to talk to you."

"Not here, son. Not now, I can't. Look, I'll talk to you at home tonight, all right?" He ushered me to the door. "I'm sorry, boy, I'll talk to you tonight."

Well, I went back to school and I was late for study period, which was right after lunch hour, but I conned my way out of it. I was worthless the rest of the day. When I walked Susan home from the bus, I told her I had a special rap session scheduled with my father that evening and that I was going to convince him to see her father the next morning and talk over the executive opportunities at International Airways.

She tried to look at it optimistically, but I don't think she ever really believed it would work. "Jeremy, I mean he's never been in the airline business."

"That doesn't matter. Are you kidding? That doesn't make any difference at all. International is always on the lookout for good men, all the airlines are."

"But he's a stockbroker, he doesn't know anything about airlines."

"Listen, at a certain level, a top executive level, switches are made all the time. Top men come into airlines from outside industries not even remotely connected with the airline industry. Happens all the time. Why? Because they know how to handle *people*. They know how to communicate. They know how to delegate responsibility. That's what it's all about."

She shook her head. "There's not enough *time,* Jeremy. We leave Tuesday afternoon—that's *tomorrow*!"

I glanced away, not wanting to hear those words, not wanting to think about them. I felt a sense of panic when I was reminded. We were nearing her apartment and I realized suddenly that I was going to cry right then, right in front of her, if I didn't get my mind off the subject immediately. I could feel my lips tighten.

"Hey, I have a terrible secret," I said, looking away from her, blinking, testing my voice.

"Oh, wow, not now, Jeremy."

"Yeah, a terrible secret. At least, it was a secret before I decided to tell you. But that's all part of a promise I made to myself very recently. I promised that I wasn't going to be ashamed of my hangups any more. I mean, why should I be, right? They're not so terrible anyway. So I thought, if I can just tell them to Susan, tell them out loud, out in the open, maybe they won't seem so—irrational. Or whatever you want to call it. Maybe they'll just seem human."

We had reached the familiar front stoop of the building near hers. Susan seemed relieved that I'd decided to change the whole mood. She went along with it, gave me the look from the corner of her eye, and sat on the steps with me. She actually seemed to be cheered up a little, which had a terrific effect on me.

I cleared my throat, frowned, the whole serious bit. "The terrible secret, uh, Susan—what it is, actually, it's painful to say, but—uh—"

"Come on, out with it."

"Uh, well, the whole thing?"

"The whole freaky bag."

"Okay, well, look. The terrible secret is that I talk to stuffed animals."

She made a soft nasal laugh and turned away, her shoulders shaking.

"Not *all* stuffed animals," I qualified quickly. "Just some that I happen to know. One isn't even stuffed, it's a hand puppet. You know, the kind you put your hand into and move his head and arms with your fingers? He's a beautiful little monkey with enormous blue glass eyes. His face is white, when it's clean, and framed in scraggly white hair and orange whiskers, and his ears stick out. He has a big smile on his face. But for some reason, he always looks sort of frightened. It's in his eyes. Not always, but usually. His name is Mickey Moto Monkey. I call him Mickey."

Susan bit her lip. "Oh, my God. Now I re—you showed him to me in your *room*!"

"Right?"

"Oh, my God." She started to laugh, the low laugh that was real, the one that sounded like a child's laugh. "Then it's *true*!"

"I found him in the duty-free shop at the Frankfurt airport when we made a short stopover there about five years ago. It was early evening, raining and very cold. I didn't see him at first, he was way down at the bottom of a pile of similar monkeys I was looking at. When I saw him, I was moved by his frightened expression. I mean, it really knocked me out, you know? I bought him, but I didn't show him to anyone until we were back on the plane and well on the way to London. Then I introduced him to my parents. He said, 'Hello,' very politely, holding his white hands together, his frightened eyes huge and hopeful that they'd like him."

Susan was leaning back against the iron railing then, smiling, her eyes narrowed slightly as if she couldn't believe what she was hearing. Even though she knew it was true. Well, most of it. Her hair was forward over her shoulders, framing her face.

"His big brother is Pippin," I went on, enjoying it, "a stuffed koala bear that was given to me many years ago —you've seen him, too. What you may not know is that Pippin is made of real koala fur, not the kangaroo fur you find on stuffed koalas these days. He's much taller than Mickey, of course, and you probably remember his big black rubber nose and alert eyes. Of lovely brown glass. I don't know exactly how old he is, but his fur's worn thin in some places from too much love. All his four leather claws have come off at one time or another and I've had to perform rather painful surgery to put them back—painful for me, that is—but Pippin took it all philosophically. Actually, he's a very brave bear. Except during thunderstorms."

That got her laughing out loud. "He . . . he hides in the closet, right?"

I shook my head. "Under the bed. With Mickey."

She laughed luxuriously, bit her lip, looked away.

"Naturally, being the eldest and all, he's very protective about Mickey. They watch 'Sesame Street' on television every morning during the school year, and Pippin explains the harder lessons with infinite patience. Of course, he has his faults. For example, when they have their friends over for parties, he sometimes gets a little bossy. Also, he's quite a snob about the fact that he's Australian. Not long ago, I talked with him about that. 'How'd you like to be an American citizen?' I asked. 'Not bloody likely,' he said in his best Australian accent. 'New York *is* our home, you know,' I countered. Pippin considered that. 'Well, you have a higher standard of living,' he admitted, 'but most Americans are so bloody *rude,* aren't they?' Mickey agreed, as usual: 'Bloody rude!' "

I glanced over at Susan, anxious to see her expression. She was crying silently, her head turned to the side, profile wet, a single drop poised on the end of her chin.

"Oh, Susan, I'm sorry, I didn't mean to."

She lifted her chin and the drop fell. "Christ, Jeremy, I—love you so much. I just won't be able to hack it alone again. Everything I—everything I saw was so—I don't know, cold and indifferent. I couldn't believe it. As if there was no—compassion for people any more. As if I was on some—bus or something, racing, speeding down some . . . and when I looked up, there was no driver any more. Nobody. No control. Then you come along and you love everything. I mean, you live in a world of your own. You know that, don't you?"

"I suppose so."

"Well, I'm deep into that world now. And they're going to take me out of it."

"Not if I can help it."

"You can't beat them, Jeremy, you're much too young. You're much too gentle. They live in the real world. You can't handle their world, you're not hard enough yet."

"I can try."

She faced me, the chin lifting. "No matter what happens, promise me one thing."

"What?"

"Promise me that you won't let them take *you* out of your world. You know what I mean? Because it's a much better one than they have."

8

I arranged for Ralph to take over my dog-walking job that afternoon, because I knew I'd have to prepare for my talk with Dad. By the time I got home, I had the whole argument outlined in my mind. I told my mother that Ralph was walking the dogs because I had an unusual amount of homework, promptly went to my room and closed the door. I wrote down my major points, memorized them, then started rehearsing in front of the mirror. After about two hours of work, the argument began to sound solid and the hand gestures looked pretty good, too. As it happened, Dad got home earlier than usual, around six o'clock, coming straight from the recording studio. But when he went into the kitchen to make cocktails, I knew it had been a rough day. You could see it in his eyes. I made myself scarce for a while. Mother and Dad talked in the kitchen until about six thirty, then Dad came out and called for me. We talked in the living room while Mother prepared dinner.

"How'd the recording session go?" I asked.

He pulled his tie down roughly and unbuttoned his

collar. "Jeremy, let me ask you something. If you were giving a recital at your school, with your teachers and students there, would you want me to walk out on stage and ask to talk to you?"

I shook my head and looked away.

"I'd appreciate it if you'd look at me when I'm asking you a question."

I looked right in his eyes and held his gaze for what seemed a long time. He looked away first, stood up and went into the kitchen. I heard the ice clicking as he made his second drink. He came back slowly, sat in a different chair and lit a cigarette.

"Dad, I'm sorry, but I've got to talk with you."

"All right, let's have it."

I glanced at my watch. He always watched the network news at seven o'clock, so I knew I'd only have about twenty minutes. "Well, I'll get right to the point. You know Susan, the girl I've been dating from school?"

He looked up at me quickly. "Yes, what about her?"

"Well, her father's—tentatively decided to take a job in Detroit."

He relaxed noticeably, took a long swallow of his drink.

"So they're going to move back to Detroit," I continued, saying the words quickly, hating even the sound. "But the thing is, her father would actually rather stay in New York, if he could find a job that was challenging enough. He wants to get into a different business and he's always been fascinated by the airline industry."

"What's he doing now?"

"He's a stockbroker."

"A stockbroker," he said flatly.

"Yeah, but he's not getting the kind of satisfaction he wants out of that job. I mean, he's an extremely bright guy, you know?"

He nodded. "I don't doubt that he is. Unfortunately, he's looking around at a particularly bad time, as you know."

"What do you mean?"

"Well, Jeremy, you know the situation in the airline industry today, I don't have to spell it out for you."

"What, you mean the layoffs?"

He glanced at me sharply. "Yeah. I mean the 'layoffs,' as people like to call them. And the wholesale head-count reductions that've been going on for three years now, and the head-count reductions through attrition, and the budget cutbacks, and the miserable forecasts that make more head-count reductions—many more—almost inevitable before the end of this year. *That's* what I mean."

"Yeah, but I'm talking about positions at the top executive level."

Dad smiled, drew on his cigarette, inhaled, then spoke very quietly. "Jeremy, listen. At our staff meeting last week, we were going over strategies for next year's system marketing plan, which we have to present at the system marketing meeting—the national meeting of all our city managers—in November. We were trying to figure out a nice way to answer the number one question asked by the overwhelming majority of employees in the field—namely, 'What about job security?' Know what we decided? To tell them the plain, simple truth. We hope there won't be any more cutbacks before the end of the year, but we can't promise that. I have to answer that question every day. I tell them, 'Listen, if you're looking

for job security, you're in the wrong industry today.' And
that goes for——"

"But I'm talking about top executive positions, Dad."

He nodded, raised his finger. "Let me finish. And that
goes for *everybody,* right down the chain of command,
from the chairman on down. Listen, I don't know anybody, any top executive in the industry today, who has
real job security. And that goes for me, too. Jeremy, I've
never had so-called 'job security' in twenty-two years in
the airline business. That's a fact. I could get kicked out
on my ass tomorrow morning—and don't you think I
don't know it."

I remember the long pause and the sound of the ice
clicking as he took another swallow.

"Would you just talk with him?" I asked, finally.

"Who, Mr.——?"

"Mr. Rollins, Susan's father."

He took a deep breath. "I don't know what the hell
we'd talk about, Jeremy. International's cut back to the
bone. Every man I know is doing the job two or three
people used to handle. That's no exaggeration. Same
thing for the women executives."

"Could you get him an interview in the personnel department?"

"Jesus, I must be——" He looked at the wall, blinking,
trying to stay calm. "I must be talking to that God damn
wall."

"I just mean as a favor to me, that's all."

"As a favor to you. What about *him*? No, what about
me? I get him an application, he goes through the whole
bit of filling it out, he goes in for the interview, they don't
have anything for him anyway, and then they find out

I've sent them a—" he started to laugh—"a God damn *stock*broker, with—right?—with absolutely no experience in the industry!" He sat back and really laughed hard, feeling the drinks, then waved his hand in apology, leaned forward and wiped his eyes. "Oh, I'm—I'm sorry, but it's just so absurd, I couldn't help it. I mean, that's all I'd need. Martin over in personnel, he'd—Christ, he'd sit down on the floor and *cry!*"

There was another rather long pause. I looked at my watch and tried to remember the other major points in my outline.

"You've always told me that top executives are extremely difficult to find," I said finally. "And that International is always searching for them."

He became serious. "That's true, Jeremy. In normal times. Today, it's anything but normal, that's what I've been trying to tell you. The airline industry has been in a recession—and I mean a serious recession—for over three years now. Men with twenty-five, thirty, thirty-five years of service have been let go. Just like that. Literally thousands of older men—their jobs abolished, in many cases. Can you imagine giving *thirty years* of your life to a company—your best years, your blood—and then getting the ax? Top executives I'm talking about, vice presidents, assistant vice presidents, directors. Cut from the payroll, too heavy a salary to carry. Early retirement, here's your pension, goodbye. Allegiance? Forget it. Paternalism? Forget it. Conscience? Forget it. Responsibility, gratitude, compassion? No way. Not any more. It was like that once, when airlines were flying by the seats of their pants, when you knew people's names. But not now. We're just too big, Jeremy, we've got too many employees and not enough money and not enough jobs to go around. A corporation isn't a human thing any more, it's a system, it's like a machine. It has to be, I suppose, to get the job done."

"The problem is, a machine doesn't bleed," I said softly.

"That's right, it doesn't. It never will. But if you want to survive in that system, you learn to work with it, blood or no blood. You change. You keep on changing, whether you like the new ways or not."

"Or you get out."

"Sure, you can always drop out. You can cop out, too, by getting into things like music and poetry and dreaming in the daytime and all the rest of it."

"Oh, man, that's just not fair, Dad."

"Not *fair*?"

"No. It's just not fair."

The conversation ended right there, because I suddenly realized it was hopeless and I felt the threat of tears. He didn't even ask anything about Susan. I called her that evening and told her I'd failed and she didn't seem surprised. She was in the middle of packing and very tired and after the first few minutes she was crying. Although I did my best to conceal it by clearing my throat and coughing, I was crying, too. After we hung up, I remember thinking about what a dumb social custom it was to drum it into a boy's head that he wasn't supposed to cry. Who the hell said so, anyway? Where in hell did my father get such arrogance, telling me not to cry? I made an angry, silent promise to myself that I'd never, ever, observe that kind of hypocrisy again. I cried at dinner that night in front of my parents, it just happened and I didn't try to stop it. I was told to leave the table. Then I cried myself to sleep, I really let go, let it all out, and I think it may have done some good.

Looking back, I suppose it was fortunate that everything actually happened so fast. There really wasn't enough time to step back and speculate about it. The next morning I went to school without Susan, because Monday had been her last day; she was helping her father and sister with final packing. I'd wanted to cut school and go over there and help, I'd pleaded, but Susan said she simply couldn't handle that. So we arranged to meet at the airport at five o'clock. Their flight was scheduled to depart at six.

I don't know how I managed to make it through that day, but as soon as I got out of school and convinced Ralph to take over the dog-walking one last time, I grabbed a taxi out to LaGuardia. I arrived at the Northwest Airlines terminal around four thirty. I was supposed to meet them at the main ticket counter, as you come in, so I just stood there and waited. Even then, my hands and legs were shaking and I knew it would get worse.

They arrived almost a half hour late, at five twenty-five, and I remember Susan's eyes when she saw me. I don't think she ever looked more beautiful or more scared. She came straight to me, trying very hard to smile. I tried to say something, anything, but I simply couldn't do it. I couldn't even smile at her. My lips were tight and trembling and I could feel my whole body shaking and I was sure she could see it.

Mr. Rollins was really rushing then and visibly upset about arriving so late. He walked quickly to the ticket

111

agent at the counter and held the tickets out. "What's the gate number, please?"

"Gate three, directly down this aisle and then to your right."

He turned to us. "Susan, honey, that's gate three. Why don't you kids meet us down there? But hurry, okay?"

The ticket agent was getting nervous. "You don't have much time, sir. Do you have any luggage?"

"Yeah, I checked it downstairs." He took off on the double for the newsstand with Susan's sister.

I remember we held hands walking down the corridor to the gate. We had to walk quickly. Everything was happening too fast and I felt out of breath already. But at least we were alone.

Susan started to speak several times and couldn't control her voice, but she kept trying.

"I decided what to give you," she said finally.

It was absolutely impossible for me to speak. I tried, I opened my mouth and formed the words, but my lips were trembling and blood was rushing to my head. And then I was angry, because even after my promise to myself of last night, I was just far too brainwashed about crying to give in, after all.

Susan understood. She reached across and pushed something into my pocket as we walked.

"Don't take it out," she said, holding my hand very tightly. "Don't even reach in there. I mean it."

When we got to gate three, it was practically empty because most of the passengers had already boarded. We sat down in the little departure lounge. Susan looked very, very frightened then.

"Just say that you'll never forget me," she asked.

I took her face in my hands, shaking, angry that she had to put it that way, angry that I still hadn't said the words. And for the first time, they came:

"How can you say that? Susan, I *love* you."

She looked up at me and told me with her eyes. They seemed happy and sad and proud and still frightened, all at the same time.

The loudspeaker boomed words that sounded mechanical: "Northwest Airlines' flight number one forty-seven, Fantail Service for Detroit, is now in the boarding process at gate 3. Passengers holding tickets, please proceed . . ."

Susan's father and sister were at the check-in desk then, looking in our direction. They were given seat assignments and boarding passes quickly. We stood up.

Mr. Rollins walked over to us, called, "Susan," then reached out and shook my hand. The grip was firm and strong. "Goodbye, Jeremy."

Even if I'd been able to answer, my voice would've been lost in the final boarding announcement over the loudspeaker, but my lips formed the word, "Goodbye."

Her father and sister hurried through the double doors of the boarding gate. It was all happening too fast. Susan and I started walking mechanically toward the gate, then stopped. Her throat made a sound as I threw my arms around her and kissed her as hard as I could. I tried to hold her for as long as possible, but she tore away from me, crying, ran to the gate and then stood beyond the doors, very still, looking back. The gate attendant closed one of the doors, slowly then the other, and she was gone.

I remember standing there completely alone, shaking and crying and still trying hard not to cry, because they

113

said you weren't supposed to. Everything blurred as I threw my jacket over my shoulder and walked back through the terminal and I jammed my free hand into my pocket because it was shaking. When I felt the cold metal, it surprised me for just an instant, and then I remembered. I didn't even have to take it out. I could tell by its bulk and the feel of the signet and I already knew what the inscription meant.

ABOUT THE AUTHOR

JOHN MINAHAN is an alumnus of Cornell, Harvard and Columbia. He is the author of three previous books, *A Sudden Silence*, *The Passing Stranger* and *The Dream Collector*, plus the translation from the French of *The Fabulous Onassis*. Mr. Minahan was the winner of the 1960 Doubleday Award.